'I want you to marry me.'

Marry him? The idea was so ludicrous, so incongruous, so impossible that Cora could only stare at Rafael, her brain unable to co-ordinate with her vocal cords or inform her feet to get her the heck out of there. Forget the Spanish Mafia—Rafael Martinez was obviously nuts. Loop the loop. A few bricks, a bucket of cement and shedload of mortar short of a wall.

Then anger rushed in on a tide of outrage. 'Is this your idea of a joke?' Or some kind of mad reality TV show where billionaires humiliated the aristocracy.

'Of course it isn't a joke.' There was near amusement in the rich treacle of his voice.

Curiosity broke through and surfaced through the haze of anger. 'Why? *Why* would you even suggest something so insane?'

'Because I think marrying you will change Don Carlos's mind.'

'I told you that I am not for sale. Nor is my title. End of.'

Finally her body caught up with events and she pushed her chair back and rose to her feet. Tried to ignore the stew of hurt that bubbled under the broth of rage. There was no need for hurt. Why should she care that Rafael Martinez was only after her title? She'd already known that. But somehow the idea that he would *marry* her for it made her feel…*icky*.

'Wait.'

The word was a command.

'Please.'

Dear Reader,

I loved writing this book because Rafael and Cora both made an appearance in my debut Romance, *Christmas Kisses with Her Boss*, and I knew they needed a story of their own.

I desperately wanted Rafael somehow to find his own happy-ever-after, even if I couldn't quite see how he'd overcome his deep distrust of love. Enter dog-loving, diffident Cora, who believes she is the ugly duckling destined to remain an ugly duckling for ever.

Another reason this book is special to me is that as a brand-new dog owner myself I managed to include a dog or two within these pages!

I hope you enjoy reading about Rafael and Cora's journey.

Nina xx

RAFAEL'S
CONTRACT BRIDE

BY
NINA MILNE

First published in Great Britain 2016
By Mills & Boon, an imprint of HarperCollins*Publishers*
1 London Bridge Street, London, SE1 9GF

© 2016 Nina Milne

ISBN: 978-0-263-26423-4

Nina Milne has always dreamed of writing for Mills & Boon—ever since as a child she played library with her mother's stacks of Mills & Boon romances. On her way to this dream Nina acquired an English degree, a hero of her own, three gorgeous children and (somehow) an accountancy qualification. She lives in Brighton and has filled her house with stacks of books—her very own real library.

Books by Nina Milne

Mills & Boon Romance

Christmas Kisses with Her Boss

Mills & Boon Modern Tempted

How to Bag a Billionaire
Breaking the Boss's Rules

Visit the Author Profile page at
millsandboon.co.uk for more titles.

To all the wonderful dog rescue charities and organisations who work so hard to find loving homes for dogs (like those included in this book!).

CHAPTER ONE

CORA BROOKES LEANT down to ruffle the Border Collie's head, and flopped down on the park bench. She adored Flash, just as she adored all the dogs she walked, but piled onto her day job, and on top of the extra accounts work, it meant exhaustion stretched her every muscle—physical and mental.

Still, she should look on the bright side—she had landed an excellent day job—an administrative position at Caversham Castle Hotel, part of Caversham Worldwide Holidays, and Ethan and Ruby Caversham were generous employers. So with her salary and all the extras one day she *would* be able to pay off the enormous debt that burdened her soul.

Determination banded her chest—she knew that repaying her parents wouldn't buy their love, or even their affection, but it would make Cora feel a whole lot better about how badly she had let her family down.

Don't go there, Cora.

Flash's sharp bark was a welcome relief from her thoughts and she squinted through the light spring mizzle at the tall, lean figure headed purposefully towards her.

Relief made a rapid exit as her forehead scrunched into disbelief. That couldn't *possibly* be Rafael Martinez. What would a billionaire Spanish-vineyard-owning playboy be doing in a park in the depths of Cornwall on a drizzly Saturday evening?

For a stupid second her heart skipped the smallest of beats. Hardly surprising—Rafael Martinez no doubt had that effect on the entire female population. Though in her case it wasn't attraction that caused the skitter effect— it was nerves. Logic told her that he wouldn't remember her—he'd shown no glimmer of recognition in the handful of times he'd seen her at the Cavershams'. Hadn't once indicated that he recognised Cora Brookes, Administrative Manager, as being Lady Cora Derwent, daughter of one of aristocracy's premier families.

And why should he? Cora had never been in the public eye. She had left that to her charismatic siblings, with their good looks and charm. She had kept her carroty-red hair, non-descript features and gaucheness out of the spotlight. Her only claim to distinction was the turquoise-blue of her eyes, and that hardly made her memorable. Plus, she and Rafael hadn't even been introduced at that one party years ago.

And yet she hunched down on the bench, busied herself with Flash, and prayed he would walk on by.

No such luck. Out of the corner of her eye she espied a pair of denim-clad muscular legs.

'Cora.'

The deep voice that always seemed laced with a tinge of amusement sent a shiver over her skin. Bracing herself, she straightened and looked up. Midnight-black hair. An aquiline face with eyes dark with a depth you could drown in. The jut of his nose spoke of determination and his jaw said the same thing. His lips charmed and allured, but his aura was one of danger.

This was a man who knew what he wanted and would take it. Not by force, but that only made him all the more dangerous—because what came with beauty was charm

and arrogance. Her family demonstrated that in spades—
and in clubs, diamond and hearts—the belief that they
could succeed at anything because it was their God-given
right.

'Rafael.'

'Evelyn told me I would find you here.'

Mentally Cora cursed Ethan's PA, but she could hardly
blame her. Rafael Martinez was Ethan Caversham's business partner and friend, after all, plus Cora had little doubt
that Rafael had charmed the information out of her. The
question was why? Even if there was some admin work
to be done on the Caversham-Martinez Venture surely it
could wait until office hours.

'Is there a problem?' she asked. 'I assume you know
Ethan isn't here?'

'I do. I understand he has whisked Ruby off to Paris.'

His deep tone was neutral, but the lines of baffled disdain on his face stoked her irritation further.

'It's very romantic.'

A shrug denoted indifference and caused her eyes to
glance off the breadth of his shoulders.

'I'll bow to your greater knowledge. I thought it a bit
of a cliché myself. But I'd be the first to admit romance
isn't my forte.'

No, but dalliance is. Cora bit back the words, though
she couldn't eradicate her frown—there was nothing cli-
chéd about Ethan and Ruby's palpable joy in each other.

'Paris is the romantic capital of the world and I'm sure
they're having a fantastic time.'

Heaven knew why she had turned into a romance cheer-
leader—her experience on that particular playing field
was nil.

'Anyway, romance is not what I came here to discuss.'

Of course it wasn't. The idea of a romance between
them was laughable.

'So what *did* you come here to discuss?'

Irritation fluttered inside her; she was not on the Caversham clock right now. Annoyance escalated as she caught herself in the act of smoothing her hands down her jeans, aware of a desire to smooth down her frizzed-by-drizzle hair.

'How can I help? I assume it must be urgent to bring you here in person?'

Wariness made her neck prickle. This didn't make any sort of sense.

His lips twisted in a sudden wry moue as he lowered himself to the bench next to her. 'You could say that.'

To Cora's surprise Flash sat up and put his chin on Rafael's knee.

'Flash—down.'

'It's fine.' Rafael patted the black and white dog; his strong fingers kneaded the exact spot the dog liked best. 'Is he yours?'

'No.'

The thought of her own beloved dogs rekindled the tug of missing them. But she'd had no choice but to leave Poppy and Prue behind on the Derwent estate—it wouldn't have been fair to bring them with her.

'I'm a dog-walker in my spare time. Flash is a rescue dog and he needs a lot of attention. His owner is working long hours on a freelance assignment so I'm walking him. He doesn't usually like strangers.' Her tone was snippy but she couldn't help herself.

'Dogs like me.'

Of course they did. In a moment of silence, as Rafael focused his attention on the dog, Cora realised that she appeared to be mesmerised by the movements of his fingers. The small growls of pleasure Flash emitted pulled her attention away and she shifted apart from Rafael, suddenly all too aware of him—the strength of his body, the way he filled the space with an aura of…of…something she had no wish to analyse too closely.

'So, as I said, how can I help?'

'Ethan mentioned he is about to send you on second-ment to another Caversham enterprise.'

Cora nodded. 'He and Ruby want to focus on Caver-sham Castle, so he thought I would be better deployed elsewhere.'

'How about the Caversham-Martinez venture? Work-ing directly for me?'

'You?' Her jaw dropped kneewards.

'You sound surprised.'

'I am. Or rather I'm confused.' She was an excellent administrator—it might not be the job of her heart and dreams, but she was darn good at it—but… 'Why not just email me and set up an interview? Turning up in person seems extreme.'

'I think it's eminently sensible. I like the element of surprise and this way what I see is what I get.'

His dark eyes rested on her face and Cora resisted the urge to squirm in her seat. The prolonged scrutiny made her uncomfortable—too aware that compared to his usual eye candy she wasn't anywhere near to measuring up. Es-pecially kitted out in mud-spattered jeans, hiking boots and an oversized hoodie, with her red hair scraped back into a frizzy ponytail. But she forced herself to maintain eye contact, to keep her back straight and her gaze cooler than iced water.

'Or don't get,' she pointed out.

'So you wouldn't be interested in working for me?'

Cora tried to think, swallowed the instinctive *no* that had leapt to her vocal cords. Surely by now she had learned not to blurt out the first thing that came into her mind? How many times had her mother sighed and wrinkled her face in lines of distaste at her younger daughter's lack of social grace?

The constant refrain of her childhood had been, *'Why can't you be more like your sister?'* Why, indeed? Cora had always wondered. What cruel fate had decreed that her twin should be so beautiful, vibrant and perfect and that she, Cora, should be so different? So average, so invisible—Kaitlin's pale shadow.

As if in reminder, she tugged at a strand of her hair and looked at it. Carroty-red whereas Kaitlin's hair was a beautiful red-gold that caught the light with magical hues. If Kaitlin were here she'd lean forward, enthral Rafael Martinez with her smile, her throaty voice and a hint of cleavage. She'd lead him on to tell her more, and then decline in a way that somehow robbed her refusal of all sting.

Well, Kaitlin wasn't here, and Cora didn't want to work for Rafael. Every instinct told her that Rafael Martinez was every bit as lethal as her very own family. Well, she couldn't choose her family—but she could choose who to work for.

'I appreciate the offer, but I don't think that is the right move for me.'

'Why not? I haven't even told you about the role I have in mind for you.'

'It doesn't matter. Really, I don't want to waste your valuable time.'

Please don't let her have put a sarcastic inflexion on 'valuable'.

'It's *my* valuable time to waste.'

His eyebrows rose, though his black eyes held more amusement than chagrin. And then he smiled—a smile that had no doubt brought more women than she could count to their knees. Heaven help her, she could see why—but she knew the exact value of such smiles. What she *did* wonder was why Rafael Martinez was wasting one on her.

A flicker of curiosity ignited—one that she suppressed. No doubt Rafael expected her to roll over and beg to work for him. *Tough.*

'I appreciate that, but it would also be a waste of *my* valuable time.' A smile of saccharine-sweetness sugared her tone as she rose to her feet. 'I'm sorry, but I'm not interested.'

The man simply sat there, made no move to stand. 'Trust me, Cora. What I have in mind you will want to hear.'

The easy assurance in his voice flicked her on the raw.

'Hear me out. I accept that your time is valuable—I'll pay you well for it.'

Cora stared at him—heard the steel under the silk of his voice, saw the sculpted line of his jaw harden. Curiosity surged, despite all resolution, instinct and common sense. This was important to Rafael Martinez, but for the life of her she didn't know why. Administrative staff were ten a penny. Yet Rafael Martinez was willing to pay for her time…

Her brain emitted a reminder flare of her need for cash. 'No strings. I hear you out and then if I don't want the job I say no.'

'Deal.'

That worked for her—in truth there would be satisfaction in saying no. In pulling down his arrogance a notch or two.

'Fine. Five hundred for an hour of my time.' It was outrageous, but Cora didn't care—she would almost be relieved if he got up and walked away. *Almost.*

'I'll give you five thousand for a day.'

'A *day*?' Once again drop-jaw-itis had arrived.

'Yup. I'll pick you up from Caversham at nine tomorrow morning.' In one lithe movement he rose to his feet—clearly her consent was a token he didn't need. 'See you then.'

Part of her itched to tell him to forget it, but common sense yelled at her that five thousand pounds was a windfall she couldn't afford to refuse. Suspicion whispered that he had orchestrated this entire encounter. And then there was a part of her that she didn't want to acknowledge—the one that fizzed with a stupid sense of anticipation.

He turned. 'And don't forget your passport.'

Rafael Martinez parked on the gravelled drive of the renovated Caversham Castle Hotel and for a scant second wondered if he had run mad—whether this whole enterprise qualified him for bedlam.

No. Resolve tightened his gut and clenched his hands around the steering wheel. This was the best way forward—the only way to persuade Don Carlos de Guzman, Duque de Aiza, to sell his vineyard.

Correction. The only way to persuade Don Carlos to sell his vineyard *to Rafael Martinez.* Because Don Carlos despised Rafael without even knowing his true identity.

Anger burned as the voice of Don Carlos echoed in his brain and raked his soul. *'Men like you, Rafael, are not the kind of men I like to deal with.'*

Well, they'd soon see about that. *Soon, Grandpapa. Soon.* The taste of anticipated revenge was one to savour, but actual revenge would be better yet. Full-bodied and fiery and with a hint of spice—like the Rioja the Martinez vineyards produced.

But first things first—right now he had to persuade Cora to join his scheme. It was more than clear that Cora disliked him—and the only reason he could think of was the fact she too disapproved of his background. To Lady Cora Derwent, as to Don Carlos, he must appear the epitome of jumped-up new money and bad blood.

That new money might be despised but it would be the key—he was sure of that. The previous evening Cora had obviously wanted to tell him to take a hike, but the idea of filthy lucre had prevented her.

A glance out of the car window demonstrated that Cora herself was headed towards the car through the light smattering of rain. She was dressed in a dark blue trouser suit expressly designed, it seemed to him, to minimise her assets, and sensible blue pumps. She looked…muted.

He swung the door of the sleek silver two-seater up and climbed out of the car; stroked the roof of his pride and joy—the glorious creation that was proof he'd left his childhood in the dust.

Not that Cora looked impressed—in fact her lips had thinned into a line of disapproval that Don Carlos himself would have applauded.

'Good morning.'

'Good morning.'

Up close, Rafael could see that her ensemble didn't just mute her: it almost rendered her invisible. Her red hair was pulled back in a severe bun, her posture was slightly slouched, her face ducked down. Perhaps it was a bid not to be recognised. Though *why* Lady Cora Derwent was masquerading as Cora Brookes was a mystery he fully intended to solve.

True, she had always kept out of the limelight, whilst the rest of her family played social media and celebrity rags for all they were worth. Nothing sold a paper like aristocracy, after all, and the Derwents were as aristocratic as they came—a family that traced its bloodline back to Tudor times.

The thought of bloodlines served as a reminder of his own and he felt the familiar pulse of anger. An anger he crystallised into purpose.

'You ready to go?'

'I am.'

Rafael walked round and swung the passenger door up,

waited whilst Cora slid inside the low-slung car, censure radiating from every pore. Perhaps she felt the car to be a vulgar show of wealth.

Yet he caught her slight exhalation of appreciation as she nestled back on the sumptuous carbon fibre seat.

As he revved the engine he shifted to face her. 'Cora, say hello to Lucille.' Another push of the accelerator elicited a throaty purr. 'See—I think she likes you.'

A very small smile tilted her mouth, and for a second his gaze snagged on her lips. Unadorned with lipstick, they were full and generous, and when she smiled he wondered why she didn't do so more often.

'You can't fool me. Or Lucille. You *are* impressed.'

A decisive shake of her head emphatically denied the statement. 'Nope. Not impressed.' Then, as if relenting, she reached out to stroke the dashboard. 'But you *can* tell Lucille that I prefer a British sports car to an Italian or German one any day. I like it that a UK designer came up with the idea, and I love it that it can compete with those European giants and come out the winner. Apparently Lucille is based on the "Blackbird" spy plane, and—'

She broke off and Rafael blinked. Genuine enthusiasm had illuminated her face and totally eradicated the dowdy image.

'You're a car buff!'

'No. My brother is, so I know a bit about it.'

Her brother. Gabriel Derwent. Super-charismatic, super-intelligent, currently abroad and off the radar for a while, following a public break-up with Lady Isobel Petersen. There had been a harvest of rumours along the celebrity grapevine of a family rift, but these had been countered by the Derwent publicity machine with assurances that the Derwent heir was involved in an exciting, new project, details yet to be revealed.

Cora frowned—perhaps in regret at the mention of her

brother, given the identity charade she wished to maintain. Then her lips snapped back into a thin line and she folded her arms across her chest.

'That doesn't mean I understand why anyone would spend such an exorbitant amount of money on a car. For the sake of a status symbol.'

'I can't answer for "anyone", but *I* bought Lucille because of the immense pleasure it brings me to drive her.'

Cora shrugged. 'I'll stick to chocolate. Cheaper.'

'But if you had the money…?'

Her expression clouded. 'I'd buy more expensive chocolate. Anyway, what you do with your money is your business. I wish you and Lucille well. In the meantime, what's the plan for the day?'

'We're on our way to Newquay airport. Then we fly to Spain.'

Shock etched her features. 'You're kidding, right?'

'Nope. We're going to one of the Martinez vineyards in La Rioja.'

'But why?'

So that I can propose to you.

Somehow he couldn't see that answer flying. 'So I can outline the job I have in mind.'

'So let me get this straight. You are paying me five grand to spend a day at a Spanish vineyard with you so that you can outline a job offer. What's the catch?'

'Hold on.' This conversation needed his full attention. 'I'll find a place to stop.'

Minutes later he'd pulled into a layby and shifted his body to face her.

'There is no catch.'

Her blue eyes focused on his face as her shoulders lifted. 'There is *always* a catch.'

'Not this time. I told you—all I want is for you to hear me out, and if you're not interested so be it.'

Cora shook her head. 'You seem mighty sure that I will be.'

'And you seem mighty sure that you won't. It's a risk I'm willing to take. It's a day of my life—if you refuse, so be it.'

'So no catch? Nothing nefarious? Everything above board?'

'No, no and yes.'

Rafael allowed his most reassuring smile to come to the fore but to no avail. Instead of bringing reassurance, his legendary charm seemed to have made her even jumpier.

'It just seems a little OTT.'

Not given the enormity of his plan.

'That's not your worry. Loosen up. Life is full of opportunities. Take this one.'

'I'm not keen on opportunity.'

The hint of bitterness in her voice didn't elude him, and a small stab of unexpected sympathy jabbed him even as he filed the information away.

'You don't *have* to take the opportunity,' he pointed out. 'You only need to consider it. What have you got to lose? Worst-case scenario: I tell you the job, you say no, and you've benefited from a trip to Spain and lunch with me.'

'Yay...'

Despite the sarcastic inflexion he was sure there was a smidgeon of a smile in her voice.

'Come on. Enjoy the day. When's the last time you took a day off?'

A long time if the slightly peaky look of her skin and the smudges under her eyes were clues.

'The temperature in La Rioja is twenty-two degrees. Plus it is an incredibly soothing place to be. Snow-capped mountains, leafy vineyards, vast blue skies, medieval villages...'

Enough, already.

An exhalation puffed from her lips and she relaxed back

in the seat. 'OK. I'm sold. But just so we're clear upfront, this won't make me swoon at your feet. Or make me want to work for you.'

'Understood.' He winked at her as he started Lucille. 'I love a challenge.'

And this one was a doozy.

CHAPTER TWO

'YOU HIRED A private jet?' Cora gazed around the interior of the plane as further misgivings heaped up. This was a bad idea. There was no way that Rafael Martinez would go to these lengths to hire her as an administrator. That was fact.

Mad thoughts filtered through her mind—maybe he was part of a drug-smuggling gang and this was an attempt to dazzle her with his wealth as part of a recruitment drive. Maybe the whole holiday venture was a cover-up. Maybe he was part of the Spanish mafia.

Maybe she should curb her over-active imagination.

'Is that a problem?'

'Yes, it is!'

Though higher in the problem stakes was the whirl of emotion that unfortunately wasn't only to do with the sheer insanity of proceedings. Ever since she'd set eyes on Rafael Martinez the previous day she'd been restless—edgy, even. The couple of hours she'd spent researching him probably hadn't helped either. Had only ensured that his image had haunted her dreams.

'Nobody hires a private jet for something like this.'

'Well, I do. Otherwise it would have taken us all day to get to La Rioja.'

Oh, no fair. The way he said the Spanish syllables evoked a strange sensation inside her and she had to force her feet to adhere to the floor of the jet. So he spoke fluent

Spanish? No big deal. The man owned a Spanish vineyard, and for all she knew he *was* Spanish.

Her research hadn't been clear on that point—it had simply told her what the world already knew: Rafael Martinez had been a teenage phenomenon, a millionaire by the time he was twenty, and he had developed a technological app that had taken the business world by storm. But right now that wasn't the point.

'But the expense…to say nothing of the carbon footprint…'

'I don't use a private jet every day. I do understand about the carbon footprint, but I also understand about the pilots who work for this company, the beauty of this aircraft, the mechanics who work on it. And I enjoy the luxury of not having to queue up at the airport, change flights and hire a car. I like the idea of not being spotted by some celebrity-spotter who then announces my destination on social media.'

The words arrested her—come to that, *she* wouldn't be too keen on recognition either. Her family knew she was safe, but they didn't know where she was or what she was doing—and right now she wanted to keep it that way. Wanted time and space to lick her wounds. More than that, there was her pride to consider. Next time she saw her parents she wanted to be in a position to hand over at least a fraction of the money she owed them.

Rafael Martinez was giving her five thousand pounds towards that goal, so maybe she should stop carping at his use of a private jet. Especially when in reality it suited her.

'Fine. I just feel bad that you're expending all this money on a losing prospect.'

As the roar of the engines signalled their departure he sat down on a chocolate-coloured leather chair that yelled luxury. 'Why are you so adamant that you don't want to work for me?'

It was a fair question, she supposed—and not easy to answer.

You're too good-looking, too arrogant, too successful, too dangerous...

Whilst true, that all sounded stupid. Then there were the fast cars, the private jets, and worst of all that aura that unsettled her more and more with every passing second.

'I have got to know the Caversham brand very well and I like working for Ethan and Ruby. I only have contacts in the company, and there is also the fact that I know nothing about wine.'

Her eyes narrowed as he shook his head at her. 'Very good, Cora. Top marks for politeness. Now tell me the real reasons. Tell you what...' He pulled his laptop towards him. 'How about I transfer your fee for today into your account now? Then you can feel free to say whatever you like to my face.'

A flush touched her cheeks. 'That's not necessary.'

'Then tell me the truth. Unvarnished. I can take it.'

There was that smile again—the tilt of his lips that somehow indicated that he knew he would win her over.

He tipped his palms upward. 'How can I hope to persuade you to work for me if I don't know what I'm up against?'

'Fine.'

If he wanted straight shooting she'd give it to him. After all, right now she didn't have to be a lady, and he'd given her carte blanche to be honest. Better for him to understand that her desire not to work for him was genuine and absolute. This was a man who went for what he wanted, and for unfathomable reasons he wanted her—Cora Brookes. Not Lady Cora Derwent.

For a second the idea held a fascination and, yes, a lure all of its own...

Time for a mental shakedown. The words *fascination* and *lure* were not apposite, and it was time to prove to Rafael and herself that she had no intention of calling him her boss. *Ever.* All her life she'd been surrounded by people like him, and for the past few years she'd worked for her parents—she knew what it was like.

'I don't like the way you think your wealth and your looks entitle you to—' She broke off at the sudden flash of something that crossed his face.

'Entitle me to what?' he asked, his voice smooth as silk.

'Entitle you to whatever you want—glamorous women, fast cars, private jets, endless favours…I don't like the sense of superiority…'

'My wealth entitles me to whatever I can afford, as long as I'm not hurting anyone or doing anything illegal.' There was no sign of a smile now, no hint of charm or allure.

'It doesn't entitle you to feel superior.'

Any more than *her* family's bloodline entitled them to do that.

'I don't feel superior.'

'But you *do* feel entitled.'

'To what? To buy a sports car? To hire a private jet? Yes.'

'What about the women?' Because, in all honesty, that was what stuck in her craw the most. 'They are flesh and blood—not carbon fibre or titanium.'

'I know that, and I'm thankful for it.'

The amusement in the tilt of his arrogant lips made her palm itch.

'I get that—but you still see them on a par with the car and the jet. As accessories.'

How many pictures had she seen of Rafael with a different model, actress or celebrity on his arm?

Rafael opened his mouth and then closed it again; a flush touched the angle of his cheekbones. 'I don't see women as accessories.'

Aha! 'Do I sense a touch of defensiveness there?'

'No.' A scowl shadowed his face and his dark eyes positively blazed. 'I don't accessorise myself with women. I don't collect them and I make it very clear upfront that my maximum relationship span is a few days and that I don't believe in love.'

Although the heat had simmered down in his eyes every instinct told her she'd hit a nerve.

'But you do admit these women all have to look good?'

'I admit I have to be attracted to them.'

For a second she saw the smallest hint of discomfort flash across his expression.

'But that would be true regardless of my wealth.'

'I think you'd find that without your wealth and looks you would have to lower your standards.'

'In which case the women I date are as shallow as I am.'

'And you don't have a problem with that?'

'Nope. I see no need to apologise for dating beautiful women.'

'What about the fact you *only* go out with beautiful women?'

'I don't *force* them to go out with me, and I make them no promises.'

'But even you admit it's shallow?'

'It's called *having fun*, Cora. I believe in fun. As long as no one gets hurt. I've earned my money fair and square and if I choose to spend it on living life to the full then I won't apologise for it.'

'So the whole fast cars, beautiful women, party lifestyle is all you want from life?'

Why did it matter so much to her?

Because she wanted to shout, *What about women like me? Don't we rate a look-in? What about those less endowed with natural charm and grace? People like me, who knock things over, say the wrong thing or—worse—say nothing at all. The ones who haven't been touched by the brush of success. What about us?*

'Not *all* I want, no.' His lips were set to grim and a clenching of his fist on the mahogany tabletop suddenly made him appear oceans apart from shallow playboy.

'What else do you want?'

'I want to make Martinez Wines a success, I want to run the London Marathon, to climb Ben Nevis, travel the world with a backpack, sail the oceans... I want to live life to the full and set the world to rights.'

Cora stared at him, unsure whether he meant it or was mocking her.

'What do *you* want, Cora?'

The question was smooth, but laced with a sting.

What *did* she want right now? A vast amount of money—enough to repay her parents for the loss of the Derwent diamonds, stolen thanks to her naïve stupidity.

What did she want from life? She wanted the impossible—approval, love, acceptance from her parents, who had shown nothing but indifference to the child they perceived as surplus to requirements.

For an instant she envied Rafael Martinez his brash desire to live his life as he wanted, by his own rules. He wanted to live life to the full and she wanted...

'I want...I want...' Her voice trailed off. 'I want to get on with my life. Be happy.'

But as she stared at him, so handsome, so arrogant, smouldering, for an instant she wanted him—wanted to be one of those gorgeous women he was attracted to. She wanted, coveted, *yearned* for Kaitlin's looks and her presence—that elusive 'It' factor her sister possessed in abundance. How shallow was that? Clearly the atmosphere was affecting her and it was time to get a grip.

'Are you happy now?' he asked. 'Do you enjoy being an administrator?'

'It's what I need to do.'

It had been a cry for approval. Another step on her

quest to be a useful daughter. She had slogged through a business studies degree and offered to help manage the Derwent estate. Had been doing just that when she had messed up—big-time. Following the diamond heist her parents had told her they could no longer trust her to carry out her job 'with any level of competence'. The memory of the ice-cold disdain in her mother's tone brought back a rush of humiliation and guilt. Reminded her of her imperative need to repay her debt.

'It pays the bills.'

Her minimal bills. For an instant the depressing contents of her weekly supermarket shop paraded before her eyes. Every spare penny put aside.

For a second a look of puzzlement crossed his face as he surveyed her. 'Well, the role I have on offer will definitely help with that. *If* you can get over your prejudice.'

'What prejudice?'

'The "I can't work for you because I disapprove of your lifestyle" prejudice.'

'It's not a prejudice. It's a principle.'

'No it's not. A principle is when you don't do something for moral reasons. Working for me wouldn't be immoral. So…' His voice was deep, serious, seductive. 'Promise you'll hear me out.'

'I'll hear you out,' she heard herself say, even as cautionary bells clamoured in her ears. *Fool.* Last time she'd heard someone out it had ended in disaster. A pseudo-journalist who had turned out to be a conman extraordinaire and had stolen the Derwent diamonds.

Turning, she stared out of the window as the turquoise sky and the scud of white clouds receded and the airport loomed.

Rafael led the way out of the small airport, glanced round and spotted Tomás and his pick-up truck. 'There's our ride.'

Cora's blue eyes widened in exaggerated surprise. 'And here was me expecting nothing less than a limo.'

'Tomás loves that truck like a child. In fact, according to his wife María he loves it *more* than he loves his children. Tomás is a great guy—he has worked at the vineyard his whole life, as his father did before him. I was lucky he and María agreed to stay on when I bought it.'

It had been touch and go—Tomás had deeply disapproved of the sale and hadn't believed Rafael was serious. Yet he had given him a chance to prove himself.

'He brings knowledge better than the most cutting edge technology and most importantly he loves the grapes, the soil, the very essence of the wine.' Rafael set off towards the truck. 'He is, however, the embodiment of the word taciturn, and doesn't speak much English, so don't be offended by him and try and remember he is a valued Martinez employee.'

Cora frowned. 'What do you think I'll do?'

Fair question. He bit back the answer that sprang to his lips. In truth he had been worried that she would look down her haughty, aristocratic nose at the hired help. Only Cora's nose was more retroussé style and…and maybe he was at risk of being a touch stereotypical. Aristocratic did not have to equal Don Carlos.

'Hey, boss.' Tomás's grizzled face relaxed into a fraction of a smile as they reached the car.

'Tomás. This is Cora. Cora—Tomás.'

Cora stepped forward and touched the bonnet of the truck, then bestowed a friendly smile on Tomás. Rafael's eyes snagged right on her lips and a funny little awareness fluttered—he'd like Cora to smile at *him* like that.

'This is wonderful,' she said, and turned to Rafael. 'Could you tell him that I'm truly impressed? It's better than a limo—this is a classic. I didn't know there were any pick-ups this age on the road any more. And it's immaculate.'

Rafael translated, and blinked as the old man's weather-beaten face cracked a genuine smile. One forty-five-minute journey later and, despite the language barrier, it was clear that Tomás and Cora had struck up a definite rapport. Tomás even went so far as to smile again in farewell as he entered the white villa he and María shared on the outskirts of the vineyard he loved.

'So.' Rafael gestured around, filled with a familiar sense of pride. 'How about a tour?'

As she stood there in the shapeless blue suit, her face tipped up to the sun, Rafael could almost see its rays and the sultry Spanish air spin its magic.

'Sounds great.' Cora inhaled deeply. 'It's incredible. It smells like…sun-kissed melons mingled with a slice of fresh green apple and—' She broke off and gave a delicious gurgle of laughter. 'Listen to me! The vines have gone to my head. Honestly, I could almost get tipsy on the smell alone. But they don't smell like grapes.'

Rafael glanced down at her face and a strange little jab of emotion kicked at his ribcage. Cora looked genuinely entranced—the most relaxed he'd ever seen her. Almost as if she'd decided to lay aside her burdens and the prickle of suspicion for a few moments. The sun glinted off the colour of her hair. It was a hue he'd never seen anywhere, as if woven by fairies.

He blinked. *What? As if what by what?* There clearly was a spell in the air.

Focus on the vines, Rafael.

'I think of it as the scent of anticipation and wonder… the whole vineyard is on the brink of what will eventually lead to this year's harvest.'

'So how does it work? I always imagine a vineyard looking as it does just before harvest.'

'Most people do, but this is a special time too. Bloom time.' Rafael halted. 'It's when the developing grape clusters actually flower, get fertilised. Look.'

He pushed aside a saucer-sized vine leaf and beckoned Cora closer to see the thumb's-length yellow-green nub, wreathed with a crown of cream-coloured threadlike petals. A step brought her right next to him and she leant forward to smell the cluster.

His throat tightened and his lungs squeezed at her nearness, at her scent—a heady mix of vanilla with a blueberry overtone. Her bowed head was so close he felt an insane urge to stroke the sure-to-be-silky strands of hair. The drone of a bumblebee, the heat of the sun on the back of his neck seemed intensified—and then she stepped back and the spell broke. Reality interceded. There was no room for attraction here.

The whole moment had been an illusion, a strange misfiring of his synapses—no more. Maybe brought on by the importance of his mission.

Her face flushed as she looked up at him. 'The smell is…intoxicating. You should work out a way to sell it. So tell me—what happens next?'

He wanted to pull her into his arms and kiss her.

The unexpected thought made him step away. Fast. 'You really want to know?'

'Yes.'

Fifteen minutes later Rafael broke off—at this rate he'd bore her comatose. Which would *not* further his plan at all. Yet Cora's interest seemed genuine—the questions she asked were pertinent and proof of that.

'Sorry. I get a bit carried away.'

She shook her head, the crease in her forehead in contrast to the small smile on her lips. 'It's fascinating. I didn't realise that you were so passionate about the whole process.'

'How can I not be? The whole process is magical. Though I've made sure we have the best technology too. I truly believe that the mix of the traditional and the new works. It took me a while to convince Tomás, but I've even brought him round. So it's a combination of his eye and modern technology that picks the grapes.'

'So you're involved the whole time?'

'Absolutely.'

'To be honest, I assumed it was a hobby for you. You know…kind of like most people buy a bottle of wine you bought a vineyard. But it sounds like you care.'

'Of course I do. These vineyards are people's livelihoods, and they have been here for years—in some cases for centuries. But it's more than that—this is a job I love.'

'More than you loved being a global CEO? More than you love your lifestyle?'

'Yes. The whole CEO gig wasn't me. Too much time spent in boardrooms. It was restrictive. I mean, I loved it that I invented an app that took the world by storm, but after a while it was all about marketing and shares and advertising and I knew it was time to sell.'

'So why do you think the wine business will be any different?'

'Maybe it won't be.'

'So if times get tough or you get bored you'll just move on?'

Cora's lips were pursed in what looked to be yet more disapproval, yet he'd swear there was a hint of wistfulness in her voice. He shrugged. 'Why not? Life is too short.'

'But surely some things are worth sticking around for?'

If so he hadn't found them yet, and he'd make no apology for the way he lived his life.

His mother's life had been wasted—years of apathy and might-have-beens because she had never got over his father's betrayal. At his father's behest Ramon de Guzman of the house of Aiza had deceived and then abandoned Rafael's mother, and Emma Martinez had never recovered—hadn't been able to live her life as it should have been lived. Until it had been too late—when the diagnosis of terminal illness had jolted her into a fervent desire to pack years of life into her last remaining months.

The thought darkened his mood, and it was only lightened by the idea of winning restitution in his mother's name.

Once Don Carlos sold him the vineyard, Rafael would tell him the truth. That he had sold his precious Aiza land to his own illegitimate grandson, whom he had once named the tainted son of a whore. Don Carlos and his son Ramon would seethe with humiliation and Rafael would watch with pleasure.

'Come on. Lunch should be ready.'

Time to get this show on the road.

CHAPTER THREE

As CORA WALKED through the beauty of the flowering vines curiosity swirled with anticipation. Over lunch presumably Rafael would outline the role he had in mind for her, and she had to concede he'd played his hand well.

The vineyard had enticed her with its scents and its atmosphere, and in the glorious heat of the Spanish sun it would be hard to refuse whatever he offered. But she would—because she knew with deep-seated certainty that whatever Rafael offered there would be a catch—a veritable tangle of strings attached. As the saying went, there was no such thing as a free lunch—let alone a lunch you were being paid thousands to eat.

Plus—she might as well be honest—it wasn't only the vineyard that exerted heady temptation. It was Rafael himself. Her prejudices against Rafael Martinez seemed to be in the process of disintegration. After her harangue on the plane about his lifestyle the very last thing she had expected was what she'd seen on the vineyard tour.

Rafael took his wine seriously—he'd spoken of the grapes with passion and a deep knowledge—and it was also clear that he had ethics and environmental morals she couldn't fault.

But, be that as it might, it didn't alter the fact that Rafael Martinez was dangerous. Because there had been mo-

ments when her heart had skipped a beat and his proximity
had made her shiver despite the heat of the Mediterranean
sun. Made her believe that all those beautiful glamorous
women might well count themselves lucky.

The thought made her blood simmer. How could she, of
all people, be at even the smallest risk of attraction? Rafael was like both her siblings—he only dallied with the
beautiful and all he touched turned to gold. Cora was ordinary and average and went pink in the sunshine. Plus,
she disapproved of his lifestyle, for heaven's sake.

As they approached the cool white villa a small plump
woman bustled towards them, a beaming smile on her
face as she surveyed Cora, and burst into a stream of vol-
uble Spanish.

'This is María—Tomás's wife,' Rafael said.

Cora returned the smile, though a sudden hint of wariness made her hackles rise as María continued to speak,
gestured to Cora, and then wagged her finger at Rafael,
whose tautened jaw surely indicated a smidgeon of tension?

'Is everything OK?' Cora asked.

'Yes. María seems to feel that you are probably a bit
hot and uncomfortable in a suit and is giving me a hard
time for not telling you I was bringing you to Spain. She
would like to give you a dress.'

Another torrent of Spanish.

'María says you mustn't worry. It is not *her* clothes she
is offering.'

María chuckled and waved her hands.

'She says once she was as slim as you, but that the years
have not been good to her.'

Cora shook her head. 'Tell her I am more scrawny than
slim, and that if I look half as good as her in twenty years
I will be a happy woman.'

'Her daughter owns a clothes store in Laguardia and

there is some of her stock here. María insists you change so you can eat the lunch she has prepared in comfort.'

'Um…' Cora looked down at her suit. 'It feels a bit unprofessional to change, but I don't want María to think I don't appreciate her kindness.'

And she *was* hot, and it would be a relief to clear her head of all foolish thoughts of attraction and temptation.

'Come, come.'

The plump woman gestured and Cora followed her into the welcome cool of the whitewashed villa.

María smiled at her, a smile that took away the disapproval indicated by a wag of her finger as she gestured at Cora's suit. 'Not right,' she said. *'Un día especial.'*

Cora frowned. A special day? Was that what María meant?

The question was forgotten as María led her into a small bedroom, opened a large wardrobe and pulled out a brand-new dress. *'Perfecto,'* she announced, in a tone that brooked no denial.

Though denial flooded Cora's system. The T-shirt-style dress was vividly patterned with a butterfly motif. Bright, bold and eye-catching, it represented everything Cora avoided in her wardrobe.

'Um…'

María beamed. *'Perfecto,'* she repeated. 'Rafael. He love.'

The thumbs-up sign that accompanied the words did little to assuage Cora's sense of panic. Clearly María had grasped the wrong end of the stick. But how could she vault the language barrier and explain that really Rafael's opinion of the dress meant less than nothing? That she was here on a strictly professional footing?

What really mattered right now was the fact that she could not wear the dress. It was the sort of dress that Kaitlin would pull off, no problem—but Kaitlin would look good in a bin bag. The point was the dress did *not* constitute 'professional'.

But as she looked at María's beaming face Cora managed to manufacture a smile and nodded. 'Thank you.'

No need to panic, she told herself as María left the room. How bad could it be?

Ten minutes later Cora had the answer. Pretty darn bad. Self-consciousness swamped her, along with a dose of discomfort in the knowledge that there was way more of her on show than she felt the world deserved to see.

The door opened and María bustled in. *'Bella!'* She handed over a pair of jewelled flip-flops and a sun hat and gestured for Cora to follow her.

Minutes later they approached a paved mosaic courtyard, dappled with sun and shadow and awash with the smell of flowering grapes, the aromatic smell of spices and the tang of olives.

Cora's legs gave a sudden wobble as Rafael rose from a wooden chair and any last vestige of confidence soared away. No man had the right to look so good. His rolled up shirtsleeves exposed tanned forearms that made the breath hitch in her throat, and as her gaze travelled up his body her eyes drank in the breadth of his chest, the column of his throat, and the sheer arrogant strength of his features.

María said something and then turned to walk away. From somewhere Cora found her voice and a smile and said, *'Gracias,'* before turning back to Rafael. From somewhere she found the courage to stand tall, not to tug the hem of the wretched dress down.

Something flashed across his dark eyes: surprise and a flicker of heat that made her heart thud against her ribcage.

'That looks way more comfortable,' he said eventually.

Comfortable? She must have imagined that flicker—

of course she had. She was not Rafael's type and best she remembered that she didn't even *want* to be.

'It is,' she said coolly, and headed to the table—at least once she was sitting down the dress would be less obvious.

But before she could take a seat her gaze alighted on the table and she came to a halt. Crystal glasses gleamed, and a cut-glass vase of beautifully arranged flowers sat next to a silver wine cooler amidst an array of dishes that smelt to die for. This didn't look like a business lunch—and it didn't *feel* like a business lunch.

But what else could it be? Maybe this was the billionaire version. But María's words echoed in her brain. *'Un dia especial.'*

'This looks incredible.'

'I asked María to produce some regional specialities. We have *piquillo* peppers, wood-roasted and then dipped in batter and fried. Plus the same peppers stuffed with lamb. And white asparagus, whose shoots never see sunlight—which makes them incredibly tender. And one of my favourites—*patatas riojanas*—cooked with chorizo and smoky paprika. And *chuletas a la riojana*—perfectly grilled lamb chops over vine cuttings.'

A special meal for a special day?

'Is this how you usually entertain your business guests?'

'No. I don't usually give my business guests lunch here.'

'So who *do* you entertain here?'

'No one. I don't bring my dates here either.'

'So why me? Why have you brought me here?'

Wrapping one arm round her waist, she tried to subdue the prickle of apprehension as she awaited his answer.

Crunch time, and a small droplet of moisture beaded his neck as he surveyed Cora's body language. Doubt whispered as he considered his own. He had not anticipated an attraction factor. In all the times he'd seen Cora at Caversham's he'd noticed her, been intrigued by the itch of memory that told him he'd seen her before, but there hadn't been any hint of attraction.

Instead he'd written her off as cold, aloof, and set on avoiding him. And once he'd figured out her identity he had assumed she didn't like him because of her social position—that she was a snob.

But now... Well, now for some bizarre reason his body was more than aware of her. Because it turned out that Cora Derwent wasn't cold or aloof or a snob. There was a feistiness to her, countered by the sense of her vulnerability, and he'd felt a tug of attraction even when she'd been hidden beneath that hideous blue trouser suit.

Now that she was clothed in a dress that showed off long legs and curves in all the right places his libido was paying close attention. Which was *not* good.

Especially as she was waiting for an answer to the million-dollar question.

'Well, why don't you sit down and I can explain. Have an olive. And a glass of wine.'

For a moment he wasn't sure that she'd comply, and before she sat her eyes narrowed. 'OK. But eating your food does not mean I will agree to anything.'

'Understood.'

He poured the pale golden wine for them and then settled back on the wooden chair. 'OK. Here goes.'

Cora speared an olive. 'I'm all ears.'

'So, I've explained how the wine business sucked me in—and I now own four vineyards across Rioja. You also know that Ethan and I have set up a Martinez-Caversham venture which will offer vineyard holidays. As part of that venture I want to buy another vineyard, which is owned by Don Carlos de Guzman, the fifteenth Duque de Aiza—it would link my vineyards beautifully and it is for sale. I arranged a meeting, but...'

His skin grew clammy as he recalled the churning of hope, anger and anticipation. He had even wondered if the old man would somehow recognise him—even though he'd known it would have been impossible for his grandfather to have kept tabs on him. His mother had changed their surnames and gone to ground.

'Unfortunately the Duque is...' *A stubborn old man and my paternal grandfather—although he doesn't know it. Yet.* 'Unwilling to sell it to the likes of me.'

Rafael kept his voice even, though it was hard. Each word stuck in his craw. But he didn't want Cora to garner even a glimmer of the truth. Though really there was no risk of that. Who would believe that Rafael Martinez was the illegitimate grandson of the Duque de Aiza? He'd had difficulty believing it himself. But there had been no disputing the facts in the letter his mother had left with a solicitor, to be given to him on his thirtieth birthday. The phrases were etched on his brain as if his mother had been alive to read them to him herself.

Cora frowned, confusion evident in the crease on her brow and the expression in her bright blue eyes. 'I don't understand...'

Careful, Martinez. Stick to facts and keep emotions off the table.

'Don Carlos doesn't approve of my background or my lifestyle, so I need to change his mind.'

And he was pretty sure his marriage into the *crème de la crème* of British aristocracy would do exactly that.

He sipped his wine, savoured its silkiness. 'That's where you come in.'

'Me? I don't see how I can help.'

There was a faint hint of trepidation in her voice and he saw her hand tighten round the stem of the glass.

'I'm an administrator.'

'You're more than that, Cora.' Rafael kept his voice even, gentle—he didn't know why Cora was hiding her identity, and he didn't want to spook her, but... 'You're Lady Cora Derwent.'

Her turquoise eyes widened and the sudden vulnerability in them smote him. For a second he thought she'd push her chair back and run, but instead she sat immobile.

'How long have you known?' she asked eventually.

'You looked vaguely familiar—I've got a good memory for faces.'

Probably because he had spent so many years studying them—always wondering if *that* person was his father, or related to him in some way. He'd constructed so many fantasies as a child, each more farfetched than the last, and yet none had been as out there as the truth.

'Then, when I was trying to figure out a way to persuade Don Carlos to reconsider my credentials, something clicked in my brain and I remembered that I had seen you years ago at some party. I knew exactly who you were. After that it was easy to make sure.'

Cora inhaled a deep breath. Her face was still leeched of colour but she managed a shrug. 'OK. Fine. I'm Lady Cora Derwent.'

Her voice was tight, but he could hear the supressed hurt mixed with a tangible anger.

'I still don't see how that helps you. I'm a lady, not a magician. I can't convince Don Carlos that your lifestyle is moral and upright. It wouldn't wash—the Duque de Aiza won't listen to *me*. I don't even get why you would want him to. Why not tell him to shove his stupid hidebound ideas? I wouldn't have the nerve, but I'm pretty sure that you do.'

'An enticing option, but that wouldn't get me the vineyard.'

'Surely there are other vineyards?'

'True. But not that many are for sale—plus, the Duque de Aiza made it more than clear that he would consider selling to the *right* sort of person.' With the right sort of blood. The supreme irony had nearly made him laugh out loud. 'Let's say this is the optimum vineyard, and therefore I am prepared to go the extra mile to get it.'

'Well, I'm not.' The scrape of her chair on the terracotta mosaic indicated that as far as she was concerned this lunch was over.

'Wait. You haven't even heard what I want you to do. Or what the salary is.'

Her blue eyes narrowed. 'I'm not for sale, Rafael, and neither is my title.'

'Do you agree with Don Carlos?'

For a second he thought she would fling the wine at him.

'Of course I don't. In fact I can't stand the man.'

'So you know him?'

'My family knows him. I went to his grandson's wedding a year or two back. Alvaro.'

Rafael froze—it took every ounce of his iron control to keep his face neutral, to keep the questions from spewing forth. Cora had met Alvaro—his half-brother—and Juanita his half-sister. She might have spoken with Ramon. *His father.* No—the heir to a Spanish dukedom wasn't his father in any way that counted. The man had abandoned him without mercy.

He blinked, suddenly aware of Cora's eyes on him, a look of assessment in their turquoise depths.

Cool it, Rafael. Focus on Cora.

'So if you can't stand him why won't you help me? Help the Martinez-Caversham venture? This vineyard is important.'

'I really don't see what I could do even if I wanted to help. Truly, he won't listen to me.'

Rafael inhaled deeply and said the words he had never in his wildest dreams thought he would utter. 'I want you to marry me.'

CHAPTER FOUR

MARRY RAFAEL? THE IDEA was so ludicrous, so incongru-ous, so impossible that Cora could only stare at him, her brain unable to co-ordinate with her vocal cords or inform her feet to get her the heck out of there. Forget the Span-ish mafia—Rafael Martinez was obviously nuts. Loop the loop. A few bricks, a bucket of cement and shedload of mortar short of a wall.

Then anger rushed in on a tide of outrage. 'Is this your idea of a joke?' Or some kind of mad reality TV show in which billionaires humiliated the aristocracy.

'Of course it isn't a joke. I'd be up the creek without a paddle if you agreed.'

There was near amusement in the rich treacle of his voice.

'There is no danger of that because of *course* I'm not going to agree. I mean…I—' Curiosity broke through and surfaced through the haze of anger. 'Why? *Why* would you even suggest something so insane?'

'Because I think marrying you will change Don Car-los's mind.'

'I told you that I am not for sale. Nor is my title. End of.'

Finally her body caught up with events and she pushed her chair back and rose to her feet. Tried to ignore the stew of hurt that bubbled under the broth of rage. There was no need for hurt. Why should she care that Rafael Martinez was only after her title? But somehow the idea he would *marry* her for it made her feel...*icky*.

'Wait.'

The word was a command.

'Please.'

The second word was a concession that didn't so much as make her pause.

'The answer is no.'

'I will pay you a substantial salary.'

Without hesitation he named an amount of money that boggled her mind. Shame trickled through her veins as the words resonated in her brain and flooded her with temptation. The figure of her debt flashed in neon colours—and the yoke of guilt relaxed its hold on her for a heartbeat. The salary he proposed would nearly wipe out the amount she owed her parents. Could be put towards the flood repairs on Derwent Manor. Then pride stiffened her spine. There was no universe in any parallel existence where this marriage could take place.

'Still no. The whole idea is ludicrous.'

To say nothing of stupid. And yet Rafael Martinez was many things...unscrupulous, arrogant...but he wasn't stupid.

'Wrong. This idea is an opportunity. For both of us.' He leant back and looked up at her, seemingly at ease with their positions. 'If I marry you Don Carlos will see that I have changed my lifestyle. He will also, I think, be happy to sell his vineyard to Lady Cora Derwent's husband. After all, the Derwent blood is as noble as his.'

Cora frowned at the note of bitterness in the honey of his voice. 'You want a vineyard so much that you are willing to get married? Doesn't that strike you as a little over the top?'

'No. And I am not proposing we stay married. Once the knot is tied I will move full speed ahead to secure the deal.'

'Won't that look a little odd?'

'Not if I handle it right. I don't want to risk Don Carlos selling it to someone else. This would be a very temporary marriage of convenience. The whole charade should only last a month, tops. Hopefully way less.'

'There would be nothing *convenient* about us being married.' This she knew.

'What about the money? Most people would agree that is a pretty convenient amount to have in the bank. Plus you'll be able to enjoy a few weeks of luxury.'

Cora closed her eyes, grasped the back of the wooden chair and tried to fend off temptation. An image of her parents' faces when she repaid them the worth of the Derwent diamonds seeped into her retina—surely that would win her a modicum of approval, a way back into the fold?

The price to pay: a temporary marriage. A few weeks, *'tops',* with Rafael Martinez.

Opening her eyes, she regarded him, saw the incipient victory in his dark ironic gaze. 'And where would *you* be whilst I lolled about in the hypothetical lap of luxury?'

Perhaps sarcasm would hide the fact that she was still standing there, a participant in a conversation she should have closed down long ago.

'Lolling right alongside you. This marriage would have to look real. The world will have to believe that we were swept off our feet in a romantic storm.'

For reasons she did not want to look into a small shiver ran through her whole body at his words. *Absurd.* The need to hang on to reality was imperative.

'As if anyone would believe *that.' Good.* That had been exactly the right mix of scoffing and disdain.

One dark eyebrow rose. 'Why wouldn't they? It's plausible enough—we met at Cavershams in the line of business and *bam.'*

The snort that escaped her lips might not have been

ladylike, but it was way more ladylike than the words on the tip of her tongue. 'Get real! You've admitted yourself that you don't do romance—you do *fun*.' With women so different from her it was laughable.

'So you're saying marriage can't be fun?'

The question stopped her in her tracks. Her parents' marriage was one of duty, not fun. Their commitment to the Derwent estate and the family name was unquestionable, and that was what their life revolved around. Fun wasn't part of the programme.

Rafael's lips curved up into a smile that turned all her thoughts into a fluffy white cotton ball. 'I promise you as much fun as you like in *our* marriage.'

Irritation permeated the after-effects of the Martinez smile. How could he sit there as if the whole idea of a fake temporary marriage was commonplace? Was he flirting with her, mocking her, or just having a good old laugh at her expense?

'No one in their right mind will believe the "romantic storm" theory.'

'*Everyone* will believe it. I promise.'

And suddenly the heat that surrounded her was nothing to do with the Spanish sun. Because Rafael rose, stepped around the table to within touching distance, where he halted.

'The world will believe that I have eyes only for my wife. That I am head over heels in love.'

The words were like molten chocolate—the expensive type...the type that tempted you to believe you could eat it by the bucketful and it would be positively good for you.

*No. C*hocolate—expensive or otherwise—was only good for you in moderation, and it seemed clear that this man didn't do moderation. Whereas 'Moderate' was Cora's middle name.

'It won't work.'

Thud, thud, thud. Any minute now her heart would leave her ribcage as he took another infinitesimal step towards her, his eyes resting on her face with a look so intense it took all her backbone to stay upright and not ooze into a puddle at his feet.

'Care to bet?' he drawled.

Right that second it was hard to care about anything but his proximity, the citrus clean scent of him, the sheer beauty of his lips and the look in his eyes as they darkened to jet-black pools of desire. Her lips parted and she released the back of the chair to bring her hand upwards—and then reality, mortification and the prospect of humiliation had her stepping backwards.

What was she thinking? *Acting. The man is acting, Cora.*

Something flashed across his face and was gone. 'We can pull this off.'

His words were a shade jerky and Cora forced her breathing to normal levels, prayed he couldn't sense the accelerated rate of her pulse.

'Your choice. Marry me...help me persuade Don Carlos it's a real union. In return you get a shedload of cash'

Cora tried to think. 'Then what happens? A few weeks after a massive high-profile wedding we announce our divorce?'

'Yup. We can make it an amicable split—say that we rushed into marriage and realised we weren't compatible. There will probably be a tabloid furore, but they usually die down.'

The idea made her insides curl in anticipated humiliation. As if anyone would believe the incompatibility story—the world would think that she hadn't measured up, hadn't been able to hold the attention of a man like Rafael Martinez. She would be able to add 'failed wife' to the résumé that already charted her failure as a daughter.

His dark eyes surveyed her with a hint of impatience and she shrugged. 'My tabloid experience is nil, so I'll bow to your better knowledge.' For that fee she could withstand a few days of paparazzi attention—the pay-off in parental approval would be worth it.

'Good. After that you could afford a career break, but if you'd rather return to work I'm sure the Caversham-Martinez venture could use an administrator when it launches.'

'That won't be necessary.' Because if all went to plan she would win back her job at Derwent Manor.

'Or, if you preferred, I'm equally sure Ethan will take you back.'

Her ahead awhirl with the surrealness of the situation, Cora tried to think. 'Hold on. *Ethan*. I can't leave Ethan and Ruby in the lurch. They took a risk taking me on in the first place, and…and they don't even know I'm Lady Cora Derwent… He and Ruby think I am plain Cora Brookes.'

'Once Ethan and Ruby are back we can explain our engagement and tell them who you really are. You can finish up this week in Cornwall and after that Ethan was going to send you on secondment elsewhere anyway. So you aren't deserting the Caversham ship. They'll understand. After all, their courtship was pretty whirlwind itself.'

'Can't we tell them the truth?'

'No.' Some reporter might get hold of them and Ruby couldn't lie her way out of a paper bag. 'Plus, the fewer people to know the truth the better.'

'OK.'

'So, any more questions?'

'What if it doesn't work? What if Don Carlos still won't sell you the vineyard?'

'You still get your money.'

As her thoughts seethed and whirled she studied his expression, the tension to his jaw, the haunted look in the dark depths of his eyes that spoke of a fierce need. This meant a lot more to Rafael than a mere business deal. Because no matter how reasonably he was spinning this idea—so much so that for a moment Cora had been caught up in the threads of the tale—it did not make sense.

'This is about more than a vineyard.'

'This is *all* about the vineyard. But my motivations are irrelevant—I am offering you a job, an opportunity. The question is, do you want it?'

For a long moment she stared at him, felt the sun soak her skin with warmth, and somewhere deep down inside her soul a remnant of the old Cora surfaced—the impulsive Cora, who still believed it was possible to even out the playing field with her siblings and win some love from her parents.

'Yes,' she said, and pulled out the chair, her tummy tumbling with a flotilla of acrobatic butterflies.

Tension seeped from Rafael's shoulders as victory coursed through his veins. The plan had paid off. Every woman had a price, after all, and he'd known money was Cora's Achilles' heel.

He pushed aside the small frisson of doubt. Turned out Cora was no different from those shallow women she'd dissed—cash and the promise of some luxurious living had been too much for her principles. Not that he would be fool enough to point that out. Yes, she had sat down, but she was still perched on the edge of the wooden slatted seat as if poised for flight.

She chewed her lip, and there came another wave of doubt as his gaze snagged on that luscious bow. *Again.* Only minutes before the desire to kiss her, *really* kiss her, had nigh on overwhelmed him. Rafael blinked. It had been an aberration brought on by adrenalin, by the knowledge that he was on the brink of success. Nothing to do with Cora and her absurdly kissable lips at all.

Focus.

He topped up her wine and lifted his own glass. 'To us,' he declared.

There was a moment of hesitation before she raised her glass and then replaced it on the table with a *thunk*.

'So how will this work? Exactly?'

'We announce our engagement; we organise a wedding. *Pronto.* We get married, I approach Don Carlos, secure the vineyard—marriage over. We move on to pastures new.'

'Define "pronto".'

'Two to three weeks.'

The potato she had just speared fell from her fork. 'We can't organise a wedding in that time. And anyway Don Carlos may not be able to make it at such short notice.'

Rafael shook his head. 'I can guarantee *everyone* will clear their diary for this. Lady Cora Derwent, from the highest echelons of English society, and Rafael Martinez, billionaire playboy from the gutters of London, get married after a romantic whirlwind courtship? I need the wedding to be soon—before Don Carlos sells the vineyard to someone else. Plus, a wedding shouts real commitment.'

A troubled look entered her turquoise eyes and a small frown creased her brow—almost spelt out the word *qualm*. 'Whereas this one's shout-out should be "great big lie".'

Ah. Her principles were obviously making another play for a win.

'Yes, it is a lie.'

There was no disputing that and he wouldn't try. But he didn't give a damn—he understood her scruples, but when it came to immorality the Aiza clan had graduated *cum sum laude* and Rafael didn't feel even a sliver of conscience at the way his moral compass pointed.

'That doesn't bother you?'

She'd tipped her head to one side and for a second the judgement in her gaze flicked at him.

'I totally disagree with Don Carlos's principles, but it is his vineyard to sell to whomever he wants. This plan is a con.'

The troubled look in her eyes intensified to one of distaste.

No. This plan is my birthright. This is my retribution.

The night he and his mother had left Spain was a blurred memory, seen through the eyes of a five-year-old, but he could still taste the fear—his mother's and his own. Through all the tears and the pleas had been the presence of a man who had come to see 'the whore' with his own eyes. Of course then the word had meant nothing to him, but he'd sensed the man's venom, had witnessed his delight in brutality and humiliation. Had watched those goons he'd brought terrorise his mother as they trashed her belongings.

But until recently he hadn't known the identity of the man he had dreamt about for long after their ignominious return to the London housing estate his mother had grown up on. Now, though, he *did* know—beyond the shadow of a doubt—and when he'd seen Don Carlos there had been a jolt of recognition so strong it had taken all his control to keep his hands unclenched.

'Rafael?'

He scrubbed his palm down his face and focused on Cora, whose troubled blue eyes studied him with concern. For a second of insanity he was almost lured into telling her the truth. An impulse he squashed without hesitation. To confide in Cora would be madness—the very last thing he wanted was for this news to go public. He didn't want Don Carlos to get a heads-up and the lawyers in.

All Rafael wanted was the personal satisfaction of getting some Aiza land and then telling his grandfather exactly who he was. Maybe that moment would in some way compensate for the way the de Guzman family had ruined his mother's life. Maybe the ownership of Aiza land would give him some satisfaction—he would produce Martinez wine from Aiza grapes and dedicate the wine to his mother.

'I will pay a fair price to Don Carlos, and if he makes the decision to sell based on the fact I have married a lady that is his look-out. We will be legally married. I will have changed my lifestyle. If you have a moral issue with that then now is the time to pull out, so I can find someone else. If you are on board I need you to be on board a hundred per cent.'

Her delicate features were scrunched into a frown, and the swirl of bright colours on her dress intensified the hue of her hair, emphasised the curves of her body. Cora looked miles away from the cool, aloof woman who had climbed into his car a few hours earlier.

He found himself holding his breath as he waited her response.

'So,' he said. *'Are* you on board?'

CHAPTER FIVE

WAS SHE ON board with the idea of marrying Rafael Martinez? Faking a marriage for money and a vineyard? It was a con of gigantic proportions and as such it should fill her with disgust. After all, she herself had suffered hugely at the hands of a con artist. Yet it didn't feel wrong. Instinct told her that whatever Rafael Martinez was he wasn't immoral—this was more than a business deal to him, for sure, but she knew his hidden purpose wouldn't be sinister.

Stop it, Cora. Why was she kidding herself? Her instincts had let her down before and she *knew* nothing. Everyone had an agenda. Including herself. The point here was that Rafael would give Don Carlos a fair price for his land. If the Duque de Aiza chose to sell just because of their marriage that was his look-out, and she would win her way back to the Derwent fold.

'I'm in.'

The words filled her with apprehension, and yet exhilaration zinged through her body as he lifted his glass and this time she raised her own, and clinked it against his. The sunlight glinted off the cut crystal and the sound echoed in her ears like an omen.

'So what now?'

'We get engaged. I thought we could do it here. I've got a ring.'

As he reached into his pocket a small thread of sadness tugged at her heart. True, she'd written off the idea of romance in her life, had accepted that men only wanted her for her title or as a conduit to gain access to her infinitely more desirable sister. But the cool, clinical nature of this engagement made her swallow down a stupid regret that it wasn't real.

'Is there a problem?' His words were said with a surprising gentleness. 'We can do it somewhere else if you prefer.'

'No. You've put a lot of thought into this.'

A sweep of her hand encompassed the beauty of their surroundings, the tang of the food, the smooth burst of the wine on her tastebuds. She glanced round, inhaled the glorious scents, heard the lazy drone of bees, let the sun warm her skin. Every sensation was suddenly heightened. The only necessity lacking was love; the irony was bittersweet.

'It's the perfect setting for a proposal. Are you sure you want to waste it on a fake engagement?'

'It's not a waste. Believe me, I have no intention of ever doing this for real.'

'How can you be so sure? Maybe there is an ideal woman for you out there.' After all, surely a man who had put so much thought into a fake proposal must have a romantic side to him—however deep it was buried.

'I'm sure. If I ever met my "ideal woman" I'd sprint a marathon in the opposite direction.'

'Why?'

'Because I can't see the point of setting myself up for disillusionment.'

'Maybe you won't be disillusioned. Look at Ethan and Ruby.' Cora thought about her boss and his wife—their love was tangible. 'They are ideal for each other.'

Rafael hitched his broad shoulders. 'For now. I wish them well, but at some point real life will get in the way of their foolish dreams of happy-ever-after.'

'I'm sure they'll have their ups and downs, but I believe they will sort out any problems they encounter.'

'I figure why have problems in the first place?'

'Because they're worth it for all the happy times?'

Rafael raised his eyebrows, his dark eyes wicked with amusement. 'But my way I'll still have plenty of happy times.'

'What about when you're old?' She would not let herself be put off or distracted by the teasing glint in his eyes. 'Will you still want interchangeable women then?'

'I can't see why not—I hope to be capable of "happy times" into my old age. What about you? I take it *you* hope to grow old with your ideal soulmate?'

Despite the mockery of his tone there was no underlying harshness—more a 'to each their own' vibe. 'It's not a hope I expect to achieve.' The words fell from her lips before she could stop them.

'Why not?'

'Because my ideal man is—' she broke off. 'It doesn't matter.'

'Sure it does. Tell me—it may help me play my role of perfect husband better.'

Cora shook her head 'No. It won't. It truly would be beyond your acting abilities. You are *nothing* like my fairytale hero.'

For an instant she would have sworn a look of chagrin crossed his face, though to his credit it vanished so fast she couldn't be sure.

'Hard to believe?' she asked. Of course it was. Men like Rafael were of her family's ilk—they thought they were irresistible, and to be fair to them woman and mankind had given them no reason to disbelieve that theory.

'Not at all,' he said easily. 'But I'll admit I'm curious.'

Why not tell him? Maybe it would be good for him to

know there was at least one woman in the world immune
to him.

'My ideal man is someone ordinary.' Cora took another
sip of her wine and allowed her dream Mr Right to float
to the forefront of her brain. 'Someone average, gentle,
endearing and kind.' As unlike the Derwents as it was
possible to be. 'Someone restful—someone I can trust,
and someone who loves me just for me. He wouldn't have
lots of money or be upper class or have Hollywood good
looks. He'd have a normal job—maybe as an osteopath or a
teacher—and we'd live in a lovely normal terraced house,
and he'd support my job aspirations and...'

And she'd got a whole lot carried away. Placing her wine
glass back on the table, Cora decided Rafael had probably got the point—her ideal man was as far from Rafael
Martinez as the moon from the sun. Unless, of course, you
counted the treacherous way her body was betraying her
dream man with its acute awareness of Rafael's.

'So you crave an ordinary life with an ordinary man?
Why?'

Because she had been surrounded by *extra*ordinary
people all her life and always been found wanting.

'It's not a question of craving. *I* am ordinary, and I am
good with that, and I'd like to find a man who is ordinary
too. Traits like kindness and generosity can be worth as
much as extraordinary feats or beauty or talent.' She had
to believe that—had made herself believe that over the
years when her parents' indifference had made her feel
less than worthless. 'Ordinary people have worth.' Just
not in the land of the Derwents.

'You have no argument from me. Joe Average sounds
harmless enough. So what's the problem? You said you had
no hope of growing old with your ideal man.'

'Derwents don't marry the Joe Averages of this world.
Derwents make alliances worthy of their name.'

Her breath caught in her throat at his expression—distaste mingled with anger darkened his features and sent a shiver of foreboding down her spine.

'So how will your parents react to our engagement?'

'I think they will appreciate that it's a business deal that—' *That will benefit them.* Cora stopped—she didn't want Rafael to know why she wanted the money, didn't want to relive the humiliation of the con.

'No.' The force in his voice was discordant in the lazy sun-filled air. 'As far as everyone is concerned, friends and family alike, this is a love match.'

Cora shook her head. 'My family won't buy that.' It would be inconceivable to her parents that anyone would fall in love with the daughter they considered inferior in every way *and* unlovable. The old familiar ache for parental love twisted her tummy.

'Then we will have to convince them. Will they have an issue with me not being "worthy" of the Derwent name?'

Discomfort touched her insides. 'They might...' No way would they let Kaitlin marry Rafael, however much money he had, but it was possible they might not care so much when it came to her.

'But the idea of my money might compensate.'

'Yes.' There was little point in denying it. 'But I really don't think they will care whether it's a love match or not. They have an immense belief in the worth of the Derwent name—they will totally get that you want a slice of it and that you're willing to pay for it. I told you—they will understand it's an alliance.'

'I can't risk anyone suspecting the real reason for this "alliance", or working out that this marriage is a fake. Especially given your family is connected to the Duque de Aiza.'

'But fake and convenient are two different things. Trust me—the de Guzmans don't do love matches. I'm pretty

sure that Alvaro does not love his wife. I'm not even sure
he wanted to marry her.' Both bride and groom had pro-
jected intense reluctance at the wedding, despite the cam-
ouflage of ducal splendour.

There was that expression again—pain, and a cold anger
that made her realise Rafael Martinez had a dangerous
streak.

'This is part of the deal, Cora. The world—including
Don Carlos—*will* believe this is a love match. I will *not*
risk this going wrong. If your parents have an issue remind them that I'll be footing the bill for the wedding.
That seems only fair after all.'

There was no glimmer of potential compromise. Cora
hadn't the foggiest idea why he was so insistent on the love
match idea, but… 'OK. I'll do my best. Any other stipula-
tions for the deal?'

'Yes. Whilst we are supposedly together you will only
have eyes for me. It may be a marriage of convenience, but
I require fidelity. No liaisons—however discreet.'

Well, seeing as 'liaisons'—discreet or otherwise—
didn't figure in her life, that wasn't exactly a tough prop-
osition. But for Rafael…? 'What about you? Will you be
bound by the same rules?'

His eyebrows rose. 'Of course.'

'I suppose it would hardly show Don Carlos that you
have changed your lifestyle if the minute the knot is tied
you start playing away.'

To her surprise a flash of anger crossed his face. 'That
is not why I will remain faithful. I may not wish for a long-
term relationship but I do not seek to hurt anyone. You may
not be hurt by my betrayal, but you *would* be hurt by the
media headlines. I won't do that to you.'

'OK.' *Thank you.* She bit back the words before they
could fall from her lips. *Sheesh.* What exactly was she

thanking him for? An agreement to remain celibate for a few weeks? 'Anything else?'

'Yes.' A line creased his forehead. His expression was shadowed by annoyance. 'I should have mentioned this earlier. I will pay you the agreed fee in instalments, and I will pay you the full amount regardless of whether I get the vineyard or not. On top of that, whilst we are together you will enjoy a lifestyle suitable for my fiancée and my wife. But don't get used to it—this marriage is temporary. And the fee is not negotiable.'

All her inclination towards gratitude evaporated in a puff of angry smoke. Anger stranded with hurt inside her. He didn't trust her. Yet why should he? Rafael Martinez was a man used to dating women who were after his money—to him Cora must seem cut from the same cloth.

'I get it. This is a business deal—my title for your money, for a limited period of time.' Another man after her title... But at least he had been upfront about it and had something to offer in return. Plus, the lack of trust should maybe go both ways. 'I fully accept the amount is my full and final fee, and when it comes to the time to sign the divorce papers I will do so without any problem. But I think we should have a contract drawn up—after all, how do I know you won't renege on my final payment?'

If she'd hoped to annoy him her shot went wide—instead the frown dropped from his brow, as if he were relieved to have the situation back on a business footing.

'I'll make sure the prenup covers you for the final payment.'

'How does your being head over heels in love tie in with a prenup?'

'No matter how in love I was I would have a watertight prenup, because I'd be a fool not to realise that however much I loved someone they might not love me back.'

The harsh note in his voice mirrored the grim twist of

his lips. Rafael Martinez was clearly not big on trust or love, let alone a combination.

He gave his head a small shake, almost as if to rid himself from the darkness of a memory. 'So now that's sorted do you have any other questions?'

'Only about a million. I mean, where will we live? What happens now? How...?'

'Once we're married we'll live in Spain. I have an apartment in Madrid and a villa here in La Rioja. As for what happens now—I'll give you this ring and we'd better organise the wedding. I assume it's customary for a Derwent bride to get married on the Derwent estate?'

'Yes.' His words made her realise exactly what she had agreed to, and she couldn't help but wonder whether she had lost her mind.

'We'll also need to spend this next week practising.'

'Practising?' The hairs on her arms stood to attention as at an announcement of doom. 'Practising what?'

'How to pull off a convincing double act. Even with a whirlwind romance there is some information we will be expected to know about each other.'

The tension seeped from her body—that made sense. That was manageable. 'Sure. I can come up with a table or a spreadsheet for us both to fill in, and...'

Without so much as a blink of acknowledgement he continued, 'And then, of course, there is our body language.'

'We can't practise body language.' Oh, heck—that sounded so...*inappropriate*. But panic had started to unfurl at a rate of knots. Because her head was totally on board with Rafael Martinez as anti-hero. Unfortunately her body had clearly missed the train.

'Yes, we can,' he stated.

Was it her imagination, or was there a hint of strain in the depths of his tone?

'We have to make this look real, so we need to show we are attracted to each other.'

'If you think I'm going to plaster myself all over you, you can think again.' The very thought was enough to bring a sheen of moisture to her neck and heat her cheeks.

'I am quite sure Lady Cora Derwent wouldn't do anything so crass. We need to go for the subtle approach. The occasional look of adoration...holding hands as though it comes naturally.'

'I'm not sure I'm comfortable with that.' The very words were making her inwardly wriggle with a tangle of embarrassment.

'Then you'll have to learn. Come on. Let's go for a walk. Hand in hand. And instead of filling in a spreadsheet maybe we could talk. How about we go and visit the local town? It's historic, beautiful, and it has the kind of atmosphere that pulls life into perspective.'

He'd lost her after 'hand in hand'. *Hand in hand. Hand in hand.* The syllables careened around her brain with unnatural force. *Get real.* It wasn't that big a deal. Yet she couldn't remember the last time she had held hands with anyone—a telling point about her life. Or lack of it...

Breathe—and quit the overreaction.

'Unless there's something else you'd like to practise...?' he drawled.

Great. Now he was laughing at her. Yet instead of annoyance she almost liked the teasing caress of his voice, the glint of laughter in his dark eyes. Her gaze snagged on his lips and she gulped.

'Nope. I'm good, thanks. I'm just not a touchy-feely kind of gal.' Her parents weren't tactile—had avoided any contact with her—so maybe it was a button that had never been pressed. 'I'm better with animals.'

'Pretend I'm a large shaggy dog and you'll be fine.'

'Ha-ha!'

Though his words coaxed a smile they didn't solve the problem. The problem being that whilst her ideal man was comparable to a big shaggy dog, Rafael wasn't. Her brand-new fiancé was more lion, tiger and wolf rolled into one sleek, dangerous package. *Fiancé*. Hysterics loomed, and for once she was grateful that a lifetime of etiquette lessons allowed her to fend off panic and hide behind a mask of neutrality.

'Let's go. The village sounds beautiful.'

'First we need to get engaged.'

Cora pressed her lips together before an insane giggle bubbled from them. 'Of course.' Forcing her feet to adhere to the mosaic paving stones, she watched as he tugged a dark blue jeweller's box from his pocket and flicked it open.

It was hard to keep her eyes open when the diamond cluster glittered with almost cruel intensity in the Spanish sunlight.

Diamonds...her very own worst enemy.

CHAPTER SIX

RAFAEL GLANCED AROUND at the cobbled timeless beauty of the town but for once the ambience failed to captivate him. His mind was focused on Cora Derwent instead.

There wasn't another woman of his acquaintance who would have been so cool at the sight of that ring. A ring he had believed would impress any woman. The diamond cluster discreetly conveyed incredible wealth and untold elegance. Yet for a second he had been sure Cora was almost repelled by it, although she had slipped it onto her finger without demur.

Then, to his surprise, she had insisted that they clear the table, load the dishes and wash up before leaving.

Even María, full of excited congratulations and clucks of approval at their engagement, had been unable to dissuade her, so the three of them had made swift work of the clean-up.

'This is amazing,' Cora murmured beside him, turquoise eyes wide as she surveyed the ancient stone walls that surrounded the village. 'You can almost see what it must have been like in medieval times.'

'It is an incredible part of Spain. I'd like you to see the cathedral. It was originally built in the tenth century and it's definitely worth a look.'

'Sounds good.'

'And whilst we walk we can start to get to know each other.'

Despite extensive research he hadn't unearthed much about Cora at all. Every search ended in a fanfare on Kaitlin, Gabriel and the Duke and Duchess, but a dearth of information on the elusive Cora Derwent.

'Tell me something about you.'

'Such as…?'

'Whatever you like.'

'Um…I have a degree in business studies, I worked on the Derwent estate, then moved to Cavershams.'

'Why? And why incognito?'

Cora stilled for a second and then continued walking, although he could sense the tension whispering in her body.

'I thought a change would give me a more rounded perspective. As for being Cora Brookes instead of Lady Cora Derwent—I wanted to see what it felt like.'

Rafael looked at her. There was definitely more to it than that. 'I don't get it. Why would you want to be someone other than who you are?' It didn't make sense. Hell, he'd spent most of his life not knowing who he was and it had sucked—though now that he knew the truth he wasn't so sure it was much better.

'This is a fake engagement—I don't have to reveal personal stuff.'

'You do if it is relevant. If you are in some sort of trouble then tell me.' Maybe there was a more sinister reason for her need for money than he had suspected. 'Come on—this is about trust-building as well.'

'Fine.' Stopping on the cobbled street, she folded her arms and glared at him. 'How about you go first? Show that *you* trust *me*. Tell me something personal.'

Maybe he should have seen that coming, but right now all he could think about was how pretty Cora was. The dress skimmed her body, showcased all the right bits, but it was more than that. It was the character written on her face, the glint of fire in the turquoise of her eyes. Had he got so used to women whose aim in life was to please him that he'd forgotten what it felt like to be challenged?

The silence had clearly stretched too long, and Cora dropped her arms to her sides and shrugged. 'There you go. We clearly aren't ready to do personal.'

There was definite relief in her stance, and Rafael realised that he *wanted* to know something personal about her—something more than what was on her resumé.

'Not so fast. I'm in. What do you want to know?'

'Um…' Surprise scrunched her features. 'Something about your childhood?'

Reluctance tugged at him as he pushed his hands into his pockets and trawled his memories. The first five years were hazy—he and his mother had lived in Spain in a place much like this sleepy town. Emma had been happy—their tiny house had been filled with laughter and love. Sometimes there had been visits from a smiling dark-haired man who had picked him up and twirled him round and brought him sweets and toys. A man he now knew to have been Ramon de Guzman.

But then one tragic night all that had come to an abrupt and brutal end that had culminated in a trip to the grey shores of England and the harsh lines of a London housing estate, with a mother who no longer laughed, a mother who had been crushed and broken and betrayed.

Sometimes it felt as though his childhood had ended that night.

But he had no inclination to share any of that. Instead he found a different type of memory—bittersweet, but one of his most cherished.

'My fourteenth birthday. My mum and I went to the funfair—we went on all the rides and ate hot dogs and candy floss and we laughed. A lot.' It had been a magical day—one of his last precious memories before his mother's untimely death.

Aware of Cora's scrutiny, he manufactured a smile. Realised that to Cora the memory he had shared must seem meagre at best. How could Cora understand its precious value? His mother had spent years of her life mourning the end of her relationship, waiting for his father to return. She hadn't lived or laughed until those final months of her life, when the knowledge that she had so little time had spurred her to make the most of every second. Yet the look Cora gave him now was full of an emotion he would have classed as empathy if that were possible. Which it wasn't. Cora had a childhood full of wonderful memories—the same memories that her sister Kaitlin had described in numerous celebrity magazines: horse-riding, family banquets and the like.

'Your turn. Tell me... Tell me what you wanted to be when you grew up.'

'I wanted to work with animals. Preferably dogs. When we were children we were always desperate for a dog, and finally my parents gave in. Kaitlin and Gabe chose pedigree puppies, but I wanted a rescue dog. My parents were appalled, but they'd publicly promised we could all choose so they let me have Rusty. He was the scruffiest dog you've ever seen, and he was a scamp, but I loved him to pieces. I felt so terrible about all the other dogs I couldn't rescue— some of them had such horrific backgrounds—that I cried for days. I decided that one I day I wanted to be someone who helped animals.'

'So what happened?'

Her expression was closed off, her lips pressed together. 'I grew up and realised I needed to do something that would support the family.'

Needed—not wanted. And that still didn't explain why

she had stopped working for her parents and moved to Cavershams. But he sensed she wouldn't answer that question, so he led the way to the unassuming exterior of the cathedral.

'Building started at some time in the tenth century, but over the next couple of hundred years it was repaired and rebuilt.'

Anticipation built inside him as he pushed open the heavy door and was rewarded by her intake of breath.

'This is incredible.' Cora stood stock-still as she stared at the huge wooden panelled interior door.

The intricate carvings were indeed spectacular, with minute attention to detail in the beauty of the depicted figures—the Madonna, the apostles… But again it was Cora who captured his attention as delight and awe danced over her features.

'It's like a secret treasure trove,' she declared.

'And there are more treasures within.'

The magnificent altar and the ancient baptismal font to name but two.

Half an hour later Cora turned to him and smiled. 'Thank you for bringing me here. There is something intensely awe-inspiring about its history and the different contributions over the centuries.'

'Surely you must be used to that? Derwent Manor dates back centuries.'

'Yes…I do love it, and the family history is fascinating—I used to spend hours making up stories about the adventures of past Derwents. But occasionally I wonder what life would be like if we didn't live in a show house that eats money. What it would be like not to be aristocracy—if we were just a normal family. Whether life would be different.'

Her voice held a wistful note that puzzled him.

'Different how? Surely the important thing is that you

have a family, you have a background, and you have never lacked for money. You've never lacked for anything.'

Nor had to subsist on hand-outs from reluctant relatives. His mother's family had extracted and expected maximum grovelling and gratitude for allowing them to share their roof on their arrival in London and he'd loathed every minute. It was a loathing that had made his words come out more harshly than he'd meant.

'There are types of want and need other than food and a roof over your head.' Her words were said with an intensity that matched his.

'Such as…?'

Cora grimaced. 'Such as nothing. You're right. I know there are many people in the world with so much less, and I'm coming across like a spoilt brat. I'm sorry.'

With that she turned to face the altar, but her stricken look touched him with surprise.

'Hey…' He moved towards her. 'Look at me. I'm sorry.' Without thought he captured her hands in his. 'I didn't live your life and I don't know how it feels to bear the weight of a title.'

'I…um…' She glanced down at their intertwined hands and then back up to his face. 'When you're a lady all people see is your title. It's who you are.'

'No.' Rafael shook his head. 'It's a *part* of who you are. Part of what makes you the person you are. Embrace it. It's an asset. Use it.'

'Like I am now—by selling it to you?' There was bitterness in her voice and she tried to pull her hands away.

Increasing his grip, he refused to let her. 'Yes. Exactly like this. There is nothing wrong with our deal.'

'My title for your money. At least you're upfront about it, I suppose,' she said.

Ah. The implication was there that someone or maybe more people hadn't been. 'Yes, I am. '

Her gaze had dropped to their hands again and he smiled. 'See—holding hands. It's not that bad.'

'No,' she agreed. 'It's not.'

And just like that something shifted—awareness entered and heightened the atmosphere with its heady sensory overload. All he could focus on was the feel of her skin against his, her closeness, her warmth, the tendril of red hair against the curve of her cheekbone.

Whoa! Attraction was not part of the deal. This was a fake engagement. As his father's proposal to his mother had been fake. *No.* Anger clawed his soul. There could be no comparison. He wasn't lying, deceiving or taking advantage of Cora. Cora understood the score—knew this marriage was going to be fake.

Emma Martinez had believed that the heir to a Spanish dukedom had loved her enough to flout his parents and society. Turned out her belief had been mistaken, and she had paid for that mistake dearly. But now it was the Duque de Aiza's turn to pay—Rafael had a plan to gain retribution in his mother's memory and he would not let that plan be sidelined due to an unforeseen and unwanted attraction.

Realising he still held Cora's hands, he dropped them and forced a smile.

'We'd better go. I want to get back to Cornwall tonight.'

One week later

Cora leant back on the luxurious leather seat as the chauffeur-driven car Rafael had sent to bring her from Cornwall to his London apartment glided to a halt. Their original plan had been to travel back together, but he'd decided to return a day early and Cora hadn't been sure whether to be relieved or offended.

That was the whole problem with Rafael—around him she felt unsettled, edgy, and unlike herself. But right now she couldn't afford to be any of those things. Because here she was, outside the swishest apartment block she'd ever seen, in the heart of South West London, where property sold for the type of sum that boggled the mind.

And the charade was about to take off in earnest. Because she and Rafael were off to dinner with her family in a five-star restaurant. Joyful reunion? Cora thought not— and her heart plummeted in her chest at the idea.

The car door swung open and there was Rafael.

'Hi.'

Cora climbed out and her poor confused heart stopped its downward surge and did a strange little pitter-pat. The man looked divine—suited and booted and utterly gorgeous. Familiar feelings of inadequacy trickled through Cora's veins—Rafael would fit right in with her family, leaving her the perennial misfit.

'Hi.'

His gaze raked over her and she forced herself to meet his eyes, steeled herself against the assessment in his. There was no way *his* heart was pounding in the breadth of his chest at *her* appearance.

'Come on in.'

'Um…' It felt like the equivalent of Daniel and the lions' den—Rafael's home versus a family dinner. Talk about a 'between a rock and a hard place' scenario. 'Maybe we should go straight to the restaurant.'

'We've got time. Anyway, I have something for you.'

'Oh…' His expression was neutral, and as she followed him into the marble lobby she felt that same sense of being wrongfooted again. What did he have for her? Why? Did he think she was like his usual type of women, who expected lavish gifts?

Then all such thoughts were taken over by the sheer wow factor as she took in the extent of his London home. Lavish didn't cover it—the apartment was *huge*. The lounge made her eyes widen as she took in the floor-to-ceiling windows that looked out on a London panorama. And yet the interior design was simple, minimal, with a home-like feel.

'It's beautiful.'

'Thank you. I don't spend a lot of time here, but when I *am* here I like to feel comfortable and uncluttered.'

Envy touched her for a second. The words summed him up—he lived his life free of clutter, whereas sometimes *her* life felt like an accumulation of emotional debris.

He pushed upon a door and stepped back to usher her in. 'This will be your bedroom whilst we are in London.'

Again space and light gave the room a feeling of luxury without being too overbearingly opulent. The enormous king-size bed looked so comfortable that Cora had a sudden desire to go and live in it. She would pull the duvet over her head and block out the world. Inhale the scent of the freshly cut flowers on the dresser…imagine that entry into the cavernous wardrobe would lead to a fantasy land.

'I bought you this for tonight.'

He gestured to the bed and Cora moved across the plush carpet.

There on the snow-white duvet was a dress—and not any old dress. This dress looked as if it had been spun from gold into a garment that epitomised elegant sophistication. It was exactly the type of dress that would be expected of a girlfriend of Rafael Martinez.

Turning, she saw the look of expectation on his face—clearly the norm here would be girlish cries of appreciation and who knew what other displays of gratitude?

Anger began a slow, deep burn. *Deep breath, Cora.* The man might be misguided but he had given her a gift, and the level of her rage was perhaps a touch out of proportion.

'Thank you very much, but actually I would rather stick with what I'm wearing.' The look of surprise on his face should have caused her amusement—instead it stirred hurt into the broth of her emotions. 'Unless you have a problem with that?'

His dark eyes looked over the dress she had decided on as appropriate. It was nothing like the golden concoction that seemed to call and lure from the bed, but it was good quality—a dark grey, mid-calf-length, demure collared garment. It whispered discretion and that rendered it perfect.

'I don't have a problem as such—but that dress does *zilch* for you. In fact it almost mutes you. You would look a hundred times better in the other one.'

He was probably right. But... 'That isn't the point. I will not dress to fit your criteria or to measure up to what you expect of your eye candy.'

'It is nothing to do with my criteria.' The words were said with more than a suggestion of gritted teeth. 'Part of our deal is that you will play the role of happy fiancée and wife *convincingly.*'

'So you're saying that no one will believe you would marry someone who looks like *this*?' As she gestured downwards with a sweep of her hand she focused on the anger and pushed away the hurt.

'No!' Rafael stepped forward, inhaled a deep breath and rubbed the back of his neck.

She could almost see the thought cloud forming above his head. *Give me patience.*

'No. That's not what I meant at all.' For a long moment his dark eyes rested on her in a scrutiny she schooled herself to meet. 'I bought the dress because this is the evening we will announce our engagement. I got the impression you were a bit nervous about this dinner, and pulling the whole act off, and I thought a fantastic dress might help.'

'Oh...' The anger fizzled out—Rafael was trying to help. The idea produced a funny little pit of warmth in her tummy. But she still couldn't wear the dress. The memory of six years ago still burned—the searing humiliation was still fresh. Those words still rang in her ears, made worse because they'd been said with gentleness: *'However hard you try you can't ever be anything but a pale shadow of your sister.'*

Blinking away the memory, she stared at the dress on the bed and for a crazy second imagined herself in it. A sense of anticipation caught her by surprise. A strange, feminine desire for Rafael to approve—no, to be awestruck, to see the socks fall from his feet.

Whoa. Careful, Cora.

For a start she didn't or at least shouldn't care what Rafael thought, and secondly the heavy knowledge weighed her down that the moment they entered the restaurant and saw Kaitlin she would fade away no matter what dress she wore. Better not to compete—the playing field was way too uneven. Better to melt away, be her own person, and if that person was 'muted' so be it.

Turning away from the shimmer of gold, she faced him. 'I appreciate this. Really. But I can't wear it.' Heaven knew that sounded inane and she braced herself for his argument.

'Hey...'

Before she could do more than register the unexpected compassion in his voice he had stepped forward and his hands cupped her jaw with a gentleness that caught her breath.

'It's OK. Don't look so sad. That was not my intent. I don't get it, but if you prefer your dress that's fine with me. But would you do me a favour?'

'What?' The word was a whisper. Her whole being was wrapped up in his touch, the feel of his roughened fingertips against her skin.

'Keep the dress for another occasion—another time

when you do feel comfortable in it. Because you will wow the world and the man you wear it for.'

Cora gulped down the sudden urge to cry as she nodded.

'And one more favour?' he added.

Gathering herself together, she managed a tremulous smile. 'Depends what it is.'

'Will you wear your hair loose tonight?'

Cora stilled. 'Why?'

'Because you have beautiful hair and I think the world should see it.'

As she stared up into the dark pools of his eyes all ability to think vanished. There was sincerity in his gaze—sincerity and a blaze that made her head whirl.

'I...I...'

'Let me.'

Then his fingers were in her hair, gently and deftly removing the plethora of pins that kept the heavy mass under control and as invisible as possible.

'There.'

The satisfaction in his voice stroked her skin and made protest impossible. Instead she gave her head a little shake and felt the locks tumble to her shoulders. She looked back up at him—and, heaven help her, she wanted him to kiss her.

CHAPTER SEVEN

R<small>AFAEL STARED DOWN</small> into Cora's face—she was beautiful. The realisation pounded in his brain and jolted him to awareness. *Rein it in.* Kissing Cora was not an option—because if he did it wouldn't be pretence, it would be for real. And it wouldn't stop at one fake practice kiss. This was not part of the plan.

Inhaling deeply, he released her gently and took a step back. 'We'd better get going.' The words sounded strained, but for the life of him he couldn't help it.

'Yes...' It seemed that Cora was in the same predicament, because that was all she said before she followed him towards the bedroom door.

The silence reigned, ruled and dictated as the limo glided along the London streets en route to the restaurant chosen by the Duke and Duchess. Annoyance at his own stupid irresponsibility churned in his gut. This dinner was important, and like a fool he had taken his eye off the main chance—blindsided by the unexpected jolt of desire—and had spooked Cora.

Glancing across at her, he absorbed the expressive cast of her face, saw the nervous smoothing of her dress and cursed himself anew. The last thing he needed was for this dinner to go awry—their engagement announcement had to look real.

'So, let's go through our plan of action for tonight.'

As she turned from the window to face him he could see her pallor in the shine of the streetlights that illuminated the London pavements.

'You don't need to worry,' she said. 'I understand what you expect of me at dinner and I'll do the job you are paying me for. I've agreed to play the role of loving fiancée and I will.'

'How about some last-minute tips on how to impress your family?' Somehow he needed to activate conversation, to recapture the more relaxed attitude they had achieved in Cornwall.

'You don't need any tips.'

Rafael frowned at the hint of bitterness that infused her words.

'You are perfectly capable of charming my family—especially as they are perfectly happy to be charmed.'

That knowledge still niggled him—he'd expected the Duke and Duchess to put up some resistance. 'So you still have no idea why they accepted our engagement so readily?'

'No.'

The answer was too quick and his disquiet intensified.

'But does it matter? The important thing is that they did, and they will now orchestrate this engagement so that everyone including Don Carlos will believe in it. The press will be all over it after dinner.'

'Are you worried about that?' Frustration touched him anew that she had refused the dress. 'I know you've always shunned the limelight.' He just didn't know why.

'The public eye and I don't have the best relationship.'

The tightness in her voice spoke of memories she would rather not relive, and curiosity and sympathy mingled in him.

'So I figure it's best to leave it to my family. That's why I don't need to worry about tonight—I can hide behind the rest of you.'

'You don't need to hide. Especially not tonight. Tonight *you're* the star of the show.'

Her look said *As if*, even as she nodded her head. 'I told you not to worry. I'll make sure I wave the engagement ring at the cameras—I'm sure that will dazzle every reporter into a shedload of belief in our engagement. I understand my role.'

'OK. Then let's make doubly sure I understand mine.' The press announcement would go better if dinner was a success—in which case he couldn't rock the unexpected boat of his acceptance into the Derwent clan. 'Your parents and Kaitlin will be there tonight, but Gabriel won't?'

'Correct. Actually, it's probably best if you don't mention Gabe at all.'

'Why not?'

A troubled look crossed her face. 'Because I don't really know what is going on with him.'

'You can trust me with this. Whatever you tell me about Gabe stops here. The more I know, the less likely I am to upset the apple cart at dinner.'

'I can't tell you what I don't know myself. A few months ago Gabe suddenly broke up with his girlfriend and upped sticks to go abroad.There was some pretty unsavoury press around the split which my parents stamped on but I don't know any more than that. I was working at Cavershams and I wasn't at home when it all went down.'

'And you haven't heard from him since?'

'Nope. We aren't that close, though he and Kaitlin are. But if she knows she isn't telling.'

'Not even her twin?'

'No.'

The clipped note raised another flag of concern; the last thing he wanted was some sort of family row at the table tonight.

'But you and Kaitlin are close?'

Cora shifted on the leather seat and slipped her hands under her thighs. 'Of course.'

'Is it true that twins have a special link?'

'When we were younger we did. There were times when I sensed Kaitlin's feelings, or was worried about her even though we weren't in the same place. But as we grew older that happened less and less. The last time I felt it it turned out to be a false alarm. I guess we've grown apart.'

There was sadness in her voice, along with resignation, an acceptance he couldn't comprehend.

As if she heard it too, she shook her head. 'In fact you probably see her more than I do.'

'I do see Kaitlin. But I don't really *know* her.'

Before she could respond the limo glided to a stop at the back entrance to the restaurant and she smoothed her hands down her dress.

'You'll do fine,' he said.

Within minutes they were ushered inside, and before he could do more than register the dazzling interior, redolent of fame, celebrity and an expert interior designer, Kaitlin swept up. 'Cora. Darling. And Rafael—you dark horse.'

She looked incredible. Kaitlin Derwent was rhapsodised over in the press for her looks, her poise and her sophistication. Rumours abounded about her love-life, but always in the most tasteful of ways—never tainted by scandal. Kaitlin had never so much as fallen out of a single nightclub even a touch inebriated. Yet somehow she didn't come across as a goody-two-shoes. Kaitlin was the poster girl for the aristocracy, and the smile she bestowed on them was generous and genuine—it lit up her classically beautiful face with its sculpted cheekbones and emerald-green eyes. Yet her smile didn't warm Rafael the way Cora's more hard won one did.

Next to him Cora stiffened slightly, then stepped forward into her sister's embrace, hugged her and stepped back. 'You look fantastic, Kait. Love the new hairstyle. The fringe suits you.'

'Thank you, hun. And I'm glad to see your hair loose for once as well.'

Now Cora froze, and whilst he had no idea why, he instinctively stepped closer to her and wrapped his arm round her waist to pull her close. 'Kaitlin, it's good to see you again.'

'I cannot believe you two have kept this under wraps. Cora, why didn't you tell me?'

Rafael frowned—given Cora's disclosure that the sisters had grown apart, Kaitlin's words seemed disingenuous, spoken because they were the 'correct' words to use.

'Your sister is wonderful, but stubborn—she refused to believe that I meant every word I said about how I feel about her.'

Kaitlin smiled, laid a perfectly manicured hand on his arm. 'Well, I am very happy to help you convince her. Now, why don't you both come over to the table? My parents are so looking forward to meeting you.'

Somehow he doubted that, but it appeared that Kaitlin spoke the truth. As dinner progressed the table rang with laughter and chat—the Duke and Duchess were full of charm and had ordered a wonderful meal. Course followed course, and Rafael could almost see the bonhomie oozing over the pristine white damask tablecloth.

So what was bothering him?

For a moment he let the music, the voices and smiles wash into the background of his mind and tried to pinpoint what his instinct was blaring. He knew instinct should never be underrated—his gut feelings had allowed him to fathom his mother's moods and work out the best ways and times to bring some cheer into her life. Instinct had made him his first million and subsequently added the magic touch to ensure his investment portfolio was the envy of many.

So... Now he knew that Cora wasn't happy. Oh, to outward appearances she looked the part of happy fiancée... but her turquoise eyes lacked the sparkle that denoted her real smile. The smile she bestowed indiscriminately on all her canine friends, whom he had met in the previous week—Flash and Ruffles et al. Border collie, terrier, or mastiff cross, Cora loved them all. The same smile she had occasionally graced Rafael with. But the smile she offered now was just an upturn of her lips, not the real McCoy.

Plus, she was too quiet—or rather the words she spoke were anodyne. They went with the flow of the conversation, echoes of whatever her family had just said. But it was as if she had to concentrate and consider each syllable before she uttered it.

Then there had been the trip to the ladies' room with her mother—it had been over-long, and when Cora had come back he had sensed her withdrawal, seen the shuttered look on her face. Yet the Duchess had been smiling the serene, gracious smile she was so well known for.

'It's lovely to see my daughter so happy,' she'd said, and as if in obedience to an unwritten command Cora had shifted her chair closer to his and laid her hand on his forearm.

And then there had been the Duke's jovial greeting. 'So you want to marry my daughter, hey? Sure you've got the right one?' Then a guffaw that indicated it had been a joke. 'Well, it's good for you that you picked Cora. We have higher hopes in mind for Kaitlin.'

Which brought him to Kaitlin—in truth he couldn't tell whether she was for real or not. Everything she said was either clever or funny. The idea of her putting even a little toe out of place was an impossibility, and it was clear her parents doted on her. True, they had filled the conversation with family anecdotes, but somehow, although Cora was mentioned, it was always Kaitlin who was at their centre. Gabriel seemed to have been whitewashed from the family annals completely.

'What do you think, Rafael?' The Duchess's melodious tone broke his reverie. 'Dear boy, you haven't been listening to a word, have you? Not to worry. We were saying that we're sure you won't mind if we whisk Cora away from you tonight until the wedding. There is so much to prepare in such a short time.'

Rafael raised his eyebrows. 'I understand there is a lot to do, but I'm sure Cora and I can manage some time together.'

Now the Duchess's smile held a hint of steel. 'We'll see what we can carve out. But if you want a whirlwind wedding, worthy of high society, then I'm afraid I will need Cora near me at all times.'

Rafael knew he should agree—after all it was the perfect solution. It would take the pressure off them having to play the part of happy couple, and he wouldn't have to get involved in the wedding preparations. Win-win. It wasn't as if he *wanted* to spend time with Cora after all—this was a business deal. Whatever the familial undercurrents were, if any, they were nothing to do with him. Cora was in this for the money—for all he knew it had been her idea.

And yet… Maybe it was a simple dislike of being railroaded that made him turn to Cora. 'What do you think, darling? How about you come home with me tonight and then I'll deliver you home tomorrow?'

'Um…' A quick glance at her mother and then Cora nodded. 'That works for me.'

'Good.' Rafael raised his glass. 'To the wedding,' he said.

A delicious concoction of strawberries, meringue and cream, a swarm of photographers and a limo ride later,

Cora was perched on the edge of a sumptuously cushioned, gloriously comfortable armchair in Rafael's lounge and staring out over the brightly lit London streets.

'You have got such a glorious view.'

'Yes,' he said, with a slight edge to his voice.

Glancing across, she saw that he was looking at her with an impenetrable expression.

'Whisky?' he offered.

Why not? She hadn't touched a drop of alcohol all evening and Rafael had drunk only sparingly, his dark eyes in constant assessment mode even though he had played the role of suave fiancé and prospective son-in-law to perfection.

'For lower class he scrubs up well—not as vulgar as I'd expected.' That had been the Duchess's grudging verdict, delivered in their extended stay in the restrooms.

'Yes, please.'

Accepting the cut crystal tumbler, she looked into the peaty depths and then took a sip. 'Beautiful. Fifteen-year-old?'

'A whisky buff as well? I'm impressed.'

'So am I—you may have missed your vocation. You delivered an award-worthy performance tonight.'

'You'd have been up on the podium right next to me.'

'Yeah, right. All I managed was a smile at the photographers.'

'That wasn't really your fault, though. Your parents did a lot of the talking, and Kaitlin played sister of the bride to perfection.'

His glance was way more discerning than Cora liked.

'Anyone would think the two of you are super-close.'

'It's important to present a united front.'

Time for a subject-change—she'd had more than enough of her family's dynamics for one evening.

'Just like it was important we portray ourselves as a

couple. I assume that's why you suggested I come back here tonight?'

'Partly. And partly because I wanted to make sure that you were OK with the arrangements.' Picking up his glass, he crossed the polished wooden floor and sat in the arm-chair opposite her, leant back with a frown. 'I sensed a vibe at the table—something not quite right.'

Now she really *was* impressed—she had thought the 'happy families' tableau had been deployed with conviction by her parents. So much so that in the first heady moments even Cora had almost believed it. Until the trip to the La-dies', where her mother had made the situation more than clear, and explained exactly how the family felt about the engagement. Not that she had any intention of sharing *that*.

'It all seemed fine to me.'

'Then why the need to separate us until the wedding?'

The true reason made her insides squish in mortifica-tion. 'You heard what my mother said. It's not easy to or-ganise a wedding of this magnitude in two weeks!'

'Sure. But an actual embargo on our seeing each other at all seems a bit extreme.' Suspicion lingered in the frown line that creased his forehead. 'Come on, Cora. Tell me the real reason. I don't like being kept in the dark.' His eyes hardened and he put his glass on the marble-topped side table with a decisive *thunk*. 'Did you tell them that our engagement is fake?'

'No!' Affront scratched in her voice. 'Of course I didn't. You asked me not to.' His expression didn't change, and the idea that he didn't believe her hurt more than it should. 'Look, the truth is they *aren't* happy with the idea of a Der-went marrying someone of your background.'

'Then why were they so welcoming?'

'Because they don't believe our marriage will last.' Hu-miliation seethed inside her. 'They think once you spend time with me you will change your mind.'

Her mother's words rang in her head. *'I have no idea how you managed to catch him, but there is no way you'll be able to keep him. Not with your looks and personality. So we'd best keep you away from him before he sees beyond the title to the real you.'*

'They don't want that to happen before the wedding because they want to use the wedding to generate income and publicity.'

Though she suspected there was more to it than that. Her mother's emerald eyes had held a gleam of calculation that told of some sort of additional scheme.

She forced herself to meet his gaze. After all, why cringe at the truth? A woman like her *wouldn't* be able to hold Rafael Martinez's attention for long. 'Don't look so surprised. They have a point. You don't exactly have a track record of long-term relationships. You can have any woman in the world. If this engagement *were* real any minute now the infatuation would fade and you'd move on.'

'So they don't mind marrying their daughter to a heartless bastard?' His lips twisted in a grimace and he took a gulp of whisky, as if to cleanse his mouth of a bitter taste.

'No. They stand to make money which they can put towards Derwent Manor.' Cora hesitated. 'I know how mercenary it sounds, but for my parents there is nothing more sacred than the manor and keeping it in the family.'

'Not even their daughter's happiness?'

'They don't think my happiness is at stake—after all, I have told them I want to marry you. They think keeping us apart will help with that. They want to keep you out of Kaitlin's orbit as well, in case you try to swap sisters.'

How she wished the words unsaid, but all through dinner her mother's words had resonated. *'We can't afford for him to transfer his affections to Kaitlin either—and that's inevitable. Not even the slightest taint of scandal can at-*

tach itself to her right now—not when we have our sights set on royalty for her.'

'Swap sisters?' Confusion swept his face. 'Why would I do that? I'm engaged to *you*.'

'I know. I guess it would just have made more sense for you to have tried to hook up with Kaitlin. You already knew her, she is way more your type, she's beautiful and sophisticated and she would probably have charmed the vineyard out of Don Carlos by now.'

Cora pressed her lips together. What was she trying to do? Convince him he'd done a dud deal? But she was on a roll and couldn't seem to find the brakes.

'Plus she is far better in the public eye than I am.'

Cora and the public eye really didn't have the best of relationships—right from babyhood she had given off what the Duchess referred to as 'the wrong image'. Once she had heard her mother tell a photographer to hide her behind a potted plant because she looked 'too sickly, ugly and pale'. The words had flayed her seven-year-old soul.

'I mean, why *didn't* you try her first? Or someone else? Why me?'

A flash of discomfort crossed his face and her eyes narrowed.

'You were right there. We worked together. It made sense.'

'It was more than that, though, wasn't it? Tell me. You asked me for the truth earlier and I gave it to you.'

Rafael sighed. 'At the time I thought you were cold, aloof, and not my type at all. I figured that would make it easier to be married to you. I didn't want attraction to be a problem.'

A cold churning of humiliation swirled inside her. Of course—he had chosen her because he *wasn't* attracted to her.

'Makes sense,' she managed, drawing deep for poise.

After all it wasn't the first time a man hadn't rated her charms.

Seeking comfort, she took a sip of the whisky—welcomed the burn as the peaty liquid trickled down her throat, horrified that she could feel a tear prickle the back of one eyelid.

'Hey. Cora. Sweetheart... Don't cry.'

'I am *not* crying.'

This was ridiculous—her reaction extreme. It did not matter to her *at all* whether Rafael found her attractive or not.

'Oh, hell,' he muttered.

And then he was next to her. His hands cupped her jaw and he leant forward and brushed his lips against hers. The featherlight touch sent a jolt of sensation straight through her.

Not enough! her senses screamed, and as if in response he deepened the kiss. Without thought she wriggled closer to the muscular warmth of his body. Raised her arms and placed one hand on his shoulder and one on the nape of his neck, where a tendril of hair curled. She heard his intake of breath, wondered if he could hear the pounding of her heart as her lips parted beneath his. Then all rational thought vanished and she lost herself to the incredible vortex of desire, to the feel of his fingers against her skin, the surge of need and anticipation and sheer want as she eased backwards on the sofa, pulling him down with her.

Then the sensation of pleasure was ripped away, leaving her bereft and exposed.

Cora sat in near shock as she registered that Rafael had pulled away and risen to his feet in one lithe movement. As she gazed up at him, perplexed, he scrubbed a hand down his face.

'Hell. Cora, I'm sorry... That was a mistake and...'

Mortification hit her in a tsunami—what had she been

thinking? Rafael had chosen her as his fake bride because she was *not* attractive. The only reason he'd kissed her was *pity*, because she'd been on the verge of tears like some sort of idiot. And she'd reacted like a sex-starved groupie and kissed him as if her whole life depended on it.

Given her experience of kissing was on the limited side, restricted to a few teenage fumbles and one disastrous short-lived relationship, she had little doubt that she had humiliated herself with her gaucheness. If he hadn't stopped—no doubt in horror—she would have offered herself up.

The idea brought her to her feet as her skin crawled with revulsion. She scraped the back of her hand against her lips.

'I need to go.'

For a second she registered shock on his face, intermingled with a flash of anger. Then she turned and headed for the door.

CHAPTER EIGHT

HER WEDDING DAY. Wedding day. Wedding day.

The words careened around her brain, but no matter how hard she tried Cora couldn't translate them into reality. The past two weeks had seemed like a surreal dream of wedding dress fittings and press coverage, and in a daze she'd smiled and posed and allowed her mother and sister to dictate every detail of the planned extravaganza.

Through it all had been interspersed flash images of that kiss, overlaid with the burn of embarrassment. How *could* she have kissed him like that? When he had made it plain he didn't find her attractive? Even worse was the intensity, the riot of sensation the kiss had wrought. There was *zip* doubt that she would have slept with him. Joined that string of shallow, candy floss women, accepted a pity sha—

'Earth to Cora.'

Her sister's face swam into focus and she blinked and reached for a glass of water. And now she had no choice but to face him as she walked down the aisle. Her throat constricted.

'Nope, little sis.' Kaitlin's voice jerked her out of her reverie. 'You can't risk your lipstick smudging so much as a jot. You are a work of art.'

More like a counterfeit.

Cora summoned a smile. 'You look gorgeous, Kaitlin.'

It was a wedding where the bridesmaid had been groomed to outshine the bride. In the past fortnight it had become clear exactly why her parents were so keen on the wedding. They wanted to use it to ensnare royalty into Kaitlin's train. Prince Frederick of Lycander, one of Europe's wealthiest principalities, had been invited to stay at Derwent Manor in the run-up to the festivities and photographers and publicists had been primed to orchestrate a subtle bridesmaid's coup.

'Thank you. But this is *your* day.'

'Do you really believe that?'

Cora regretted the words as soon as they left her mouth—they hadn't discussed the Duchess's plan and it would be better to keep it that way. She and Kaitlin had always had a tacit consent not to discuss their parents' differing attitudes to each twin. Had known that to do so would ruin the relationship they had managed to salvage—one of civility.

Even in childhood Kaitlin had been compliant—whilst she had never mocked Cora or been mean to her, neither had she defended her to her parents. Yet the bond of twinship *did* exist, and there had been times when Cora had found herself calling Kaitlin, and vice versa, just to check if her sister was all right.

Kaitlin sighed. 'I believe it should be. But what I hope most of all is that you and Rafael are happy together. Mum and Dad don't have to be right, you know—if you and Rafael love each other this marriage *will* work.'

Cora frowned. Was that a tear? 'Kait? You OK?'

'Of course I am. I'm just glad for you. Be happy, little sis.'

If only. Cora couldn't see so much as a glimmer of happiness in her near future. She had no idea how Rafael would be, but anger would be somewhere in the mix. Given she had ignored his two attempts to get in contact and had kept herself behind the barricade of wedding preparations. Childish, yes, but she simply hadn't wanted to face him or her actions.

But now—now there would be no escape.

Her tummy churned and she could feel the colour leech from her skin, so no doubt she was paler than the creamy tulle and lace of her gown. If only she could locate a pause button and stop events. Better yet fast forward to when the marriage was over.

Pride stiffened her spine—if it killed her she would act as though that kiss hadn't happened. Perhaps if she tried hard enough she could kid herself that it hadn't.

'Let's go.'

All she had to do was follow her mother's instructions. *'All you need do is smile, Cora. That and be gracious. Try to remember that, hard though it is to believe, you are a Derwent. Do not let your name down again.'*

So Cora smiled and posed and waved from the splendid gilded horse-drawn carriage that bowled her along the gravelled pathways of Derwent Manor. The sun had decided to co-operate and it glinted on the green-leaved oaks that edged the driveway as the church bells rang out to join the clip-clop of the horses' hooves and the light jingle of their bells. Cora smiled until her muscles ached, even as the words *fake, fake, fake* tolled through her brain.

She alighted from the carriage and posed with her father in front of the ancient sandstone church that had stood for centuries and seen the nuptials of generations of Derwents. Her father beamed down at her, one arm across her bare shoulders. The irony struck her so hard her knees nearly buckled. *Everything* about this day was fraudulent—her father had never once hugged her, and now he was playing to the camera for all he was worth.

The impulse to shove him away, to spin on her couture heel and abandon the pretence, nigh on overwhelmed her.

But as her body tensed and turned she glimpsed the tall form of Rafael through the imposing arch of the church doors. Flight was not possible—she had made a promise, struck a deal, and she wouldn't—couldn't—renege on that.

Instead she kept her heels grounded and smiled even harder as Kaitlin and the Duchess stepped forward under the pretext of rearranging her veil. Cora sensed the shifting of attention to Kaitlin with relief, took the moment to regroup and try to soothe her ever-mounting panic at the magnitude of her actions.

Then she took her father's proffered am and entered the church to begin the portentous walk down the aisle. The deep notes from the organ reverberated around the cavernous interior, bounced off the sunlit blues and reds of the stained glass and mingled with the delicate scent of the pew-end posies of sweet peas and stocks redolent of spring.

The simple beauty of the church weighted her soul and her feet in equal measure as she approached the altar and the man who had haunted her dreams. Her heart twisted, pounded and cartwheeled, but from deep down she channelled cool, tried to be aloof. Not by so much as a hair on her head would she reveal the sorry state she was in.

Instead she focused on her remit, sought out people, smiled at the aquiline profile of Don Carlos Aiza, nodded at Prince Frederick. She witnessed how few people Rafael had asked—a handful of business associates, but no family at all. She caught a glimpse of Ethan and Ruby, hand in hand, smiles on their faces, and a lump formed in her throat. Their vows had been meaningful. Hers would be worthless and the idea hurt.

The last few paces and the music swirled around her, the guests merged into an anonymous mass and there was only Rafael. Her emotions were in a tailspin as she absorbed his aura, sensed the leashed tension in his powerful body, glimpsed the ice in his dark eyes that belied the smile on his lips as he stepped forward.

Their surroundings diminished as the vicar took them through the ceremony; Rafael's deep voice was clear, confident, almost triumphant. Then it was done. They were pronounced man and wife and Rafael lifted the gauzy silk of her veil and took her hands in his. Cora looked down at their clasped hands and a host of sensations stampeded along her synapses. There was a thrill of unwanted desire alongside a disconcerting sense of safety.

'You may kiss the bride,' the vicar declared.

Rafael stared down into Cora's wide turquoise eyes and saw the hint of vulnerability in their depths. The slow burn of anger that had wrapped his chest for a fortnight dissolved in a strange ache of confusion. *Bad idea.* He needed to hang on to anger.

Anger with himself for the folly that had put this whole enterprise at risk. Kissing Cora had been foolhardy, but he'd wanted to *show* her how attractive she was—that he'd got it wrong in his belief that she was cold and aloof. One gentle brush of the lips—that had been his intent. Instead he'd released a tidal wave of desire and passion that he'd been nigh on helpless to withstand. It had taken every atom of will power to pull away from the brink.

But then he had seen her reaction, and the revulsion on her face had sucker-punched him in the gut. He had seen the savagery of her swipe against her lips, as if she had sullied herself in some way. It had dawned on him then that Cora was no better than the rest of her family, than the de Guzmans, in her inherent feelings of superiority.

Focus. Or it would be him who blew this pretence to smithereens.

Gently he tipped her chin up, dipped his head and touched his lips to hers. Against his will he let his lips linger, fascinated anew by the lush softness, the taste of mint with a hint of strawberry, the texture of her hair against his fingers, the slight intake of her breath. Something shimmered—a connection that bound them together.

Get a grip. They were connected in a business sense—temporarily. That was all. For better or for worse they had committed to this charade and they needed to see it through. Cora wanted money and he wanted retribution.

He broke the kiss and scanned the church until he found the erect figure of Don Carlos. His hands threatened to fist and he allowed an image of his mother to fill his brain, her heart and body broken by the Duque de Aiza's betrayal. Whilst he had been unable to protect her.

That was when he'd vowed to become strong—and he had. But no amount of strength had been able to heal his mother's sense of loss, nor had his strength been able to save her from the illness that had taken her. But now—now he could at least avenge her memory.

The thought carried him through the interminable photographs, helped to steel him against the Cora effect—her scent, her grace, despite the over-fussiness of her dress. It was an ivory and lace confection that she wore with a self-consciousness he sensed beneath her outer poise. He frowned—it wasn't the dress *he* would have picked for her—though he could see its beauty, the design was too lacy, too frilly for Cora.

'It's a wrap,' the photographer said.

The Duchess stepped forward. 'I'd like one final picture of Kaitlin and Cora together.'

Instinct nudged Rafael as he saw Cora's face etched with an almost stoic pain, clocked Kaitlin's expression of near refusal.

'Come on, girls—I think it's a picture the world will appreciate.'

Whatever the sisters really thought they nodded in unison, and for a fleeting second Rafael saw evidence of their twins' connection in the swift glance they exchanged. They moved close together for the photo and Rafael's frown deepened. Something niggled, but he couldn't put his finger on what it was.

Moments later the Duchess bestowed upon the group her trademark serene smile. 'On to the Manor for the reception. Now, I thought you two newlyweds would like a few moments' privacy, so we've put you in the limo and we'll commandeer the horse and carriage.'

Rafael studied the Duchess's expression and wondered if only he could see the glint of steel behind the smile. For a second he considered a counter-command but then decided against it. After all, he'd appreciate a private chat with Cora—she could hardly pull a disappearing act in a limo.

'Great idea,' he said easily. 'Have at it.'

Once inside the cool interior of the limo he turned to Cora, who had moved as close to the window and as far away from him as possible, given the sheer volume of her wedding dress.

'Are you and your parents hiding me away from the masses?'

Her lips twisted in a small grimace. 'You heard my mother—she's giving us privacy.'

Not a denial, he noted, but now wasn't the time to press the point even though the idea made his molars grind. The important thing now was the reception and making sure they pulled it off.

'Why didn't you return my calls? We needed to talk about the other night.'

Twisting her hands in her lap, she shifted to face him. 'No, we didn't. There is nothing to talk about. As far as I'm concerned it never happened and all I want to do is forget it.'

There it was again—her expression held a distaste that packed a powerful punch and chagrin hit him low in the gut. It was as though the thought of that kiss made her feel sick. His fingers clenched round his knees and he forced himself to relax. It didn't matter—all that mattered was the vineyard.

'As you wish. But don't let your feelings affect how you perform.' Anger and hurt weighted him down. 'This is our wedding reception and you need to play the part of loved-up bride.'

Her hands clenched into the froth of lace and she gave a small almost bitter laugh as the limo guided to a stop. 'Don't worry, Rafael. A deal is a deal. I'll smile my way through this.'

Cora's head pounded. Almost as if a thunderous hip-hop beat the air rather than the tasteful strains of classical music from an elite string quartet. But still she smiled at the parade of people who walked the receiving line where she stood next to Rafael, flanked by her parents and Kaitlin.

Behind them the famed Derwent Gardens were in bloom, a riot of spring colours and scents, forming the backdrop for the enormous marquees erected on the lush lawns. Muffled by the canvas walls, champagne corks popped amidst the tinkle of laughter and the chink of glasses.

Tuxedoed waiters circled with platters of canapés—skewered tiger prawns, *foie gras*, caviar-topped crackers, tiny herby croutons topped with shavings of smoked beef and parmesan.

All garnered murmurs of appreciation. It was the perfect fairytale wedding. And all Cora could feel was muted horror at the fraudulence of it all—after the clinical coldness of the past fortnight of wedding preparations. It was a wedding designed to dupe Don Carlos and entice Prince Frederick. And she was as guilty as anyone in the deception. Here she was—perma-smile in place as platitudes poured from her tongue in torrents.

What was Rafael thinking? What was he feeling? Impossible to know. A sudden regret assaulted her that she hadn't taken him up on his offer to talk. But no—there could be no benefit to an analysis of her humiliation.

Next to her, he tensed, and she glanced up at him and bit back a gasp. For a second his dark eyes had been pools of fury and pain. She followed his gaze and saw the approach of Don Carlos and his granddaughter Juanita. Without thought she shifted closer to him and upped the wattage of her smile as she faced the Duque de Aiza.

The silver-haired man returned her smile, though there was no warmth in the upturn of his thin lips or his eyes. 'Congratulations to both of you. I apologise that the rest of my family were unable to attend. Juanita—you remember Cora from Alvaro's wedding, don't you?'

The sultry dark-haired young woman shot her grandfather a look that denoted sulkiness but then nodded.

Cora stepped into the breach. 'I certainly remember *you*, Juanita—you looked so very beautiful in traditional Spanish costume, and your flamenco dancing was incredible.'

It was the right thing to have said. All trace of sullenness vanished and Juanita's face lit up. 'Thank you. I love to dance.' Her tone held the weight of defiance. 'If I could I would make it my career.'

The old man's face hardened and Cora almost flinched.

Then Don Carlos smiled. 'But you can't, Juanita. I have told you that.'

He turned to Rafael, and it was only then that Cora registered how rigid her husband's body was. She slipped her hand into his to give it a warning squeeze.

'Rafael,' the Duque said. 'How interesting to see you

again. I'm surprised you didn't mention Cora at our business meeting.'

Rafael had recovered now, his expression polite, his body relaxed. 'As you say, our meeting was business and this is personal.'

'Sometimes the two can connect.'

'Indeed.'

And with that the Duque de Aiza moved along the line.

Rafael glanced down at their entwined fingers, an unreadable expression on his face before he acknowledged congratulations from the next guest.

Then they moved forward to mingle and sample the delicacies. Cora heard Prince Frederick's amazement at the inclusion of pickled herring, a favourite of his, and her mother's melodious laugh as she informed the Prince that Kaitlin had suggested the dish.

Rafael was borne away by Ethan, and Cora felt an irrational emptiness—somehow his proximity made the part of bride easier to play...perhaps because his very aura diminished others and made them less scary.

Juanita approached her and Cora breathed a sigh of relief—she liked the young Spanish girl.

'Thank you for what you said earlier. About the dance at Alvaro's wedding. Grandfather didn't know I was going to do it and he was furious.' Her look darkened. 'Truly angry. But for once my father stood up to him—he said I have amazing talent. But he won't stand up to him further—make him agree to let me dance as a career. Just because my grandfather believes that it's beneath a noblewoman. Well, he is wrong—and I *will* fulfil my ambition. Sometimes when something is wrong and you want it very much you should disobey and rebel. Don't you think?'

Envy touched Cora for an instant as she looked at Juanita's vital, determined face. It had never occurred to her to disobey her parents or rebel—all she had ever wanted was their love, or even just a morsel of affection.

'I think people *should* pursue their dreams,' Juanita continued loudly, her eyes gleaming with defiance as Don Carlos came up.

'Off you go, Juanita. I would like a word with Cora.'

He would? Panic swirled in Cora's tummy as she glanced around for Rafael. The last thing she wanted was to mess up this vineyard deal by saying the wrong thing— a speciality of hers.

Smiles and platitudes.

'I think my granddaughter likes you.'

'I like her too.'

'Good. Then perhaps you can persuade her to follow your example.'

'In what way?' Apprehension tickled the base of her spine, and the heaviness of her wedding dress seemed suddenly magnified.

'I want you to advise her to marry money. I wouldn't want her to marry riff-raff, as you have, but the principle is sound. I have found an extremely affluent suitor of good birth for Juanita, but she is proving to be stubborn.'

Disbelief at his words vied with a surge of anger. *Riff-raff?* Was he for real? 'I don't consider Rafael to be "riff-raff".'

'Cora. You are a Derwent—one of the aristocracy. You can trace your heritage back for centuries of blue blood. Who is Rafael Martinez? I can tell you. He is of low birth, and his ancestors were no doubt louts and criminals. But he has money.'

Her palm itched with an urge to slap him, or better yet ram her stiletto into his shin. 'I am not marrying Rafael for his money.'

Don Carlos shook his head. 'I see why the "love-match" story is better publicity, but in reality you *are* marrying him for his money—and please don't think I blame you. You are guaranteed a luxurious lifestyle and you will help your family. I am aware of the pressures of running a vast estate in today's world, believe me. I am sure your father is proud of you.'

Self-loathing ran through her veins—how she wished she could truthfully tell this man he was wrong. But he was right—she was standing there in an elaborate, flower-filled marquee, surrounded by women dripping diamonds, emeralds and titles, clad in a frivolous lace dress that she loathed, for *money*. But that didn't give Don Carlos the right to insult Rafael or to make these arrogant assumptions. Yet she shouldn't be surprised—after all he had insulted Rafael to his face, refused to sully his land by selling it to a man of Rafael's low birth.

Anger flared and surged in her at the derisive look on the Duque's face, along with a lightning bolt of understanding that made her heart ache. Did Rafael want Don Carlos to believe this was a love-match to *prove* that a titled person could love a person lower down the social strata? The idea was strange—Rafael's aura of self-confidence was so impermeable—but somehow Cora knew she was right, and an urge to defend him swept over her. Much the same way she felt the need to adopt every stray dog.

'Actually, I don't feel I *am* marrying beneath me—I admire what Rafael has achieved, his work ethic and the way he has made such an incredible success of his life through his own efforts. As for my title—I did nothing to earn it. I simply inherited it.'

Cora came to a sudden stop; she was supposed to help charm this man into giving up a vineyard. *Smiles and platitudes, remember?*

But Don Carlos simply looked amused. 'But it's what comes *with* the title, Cora. It is the heritage, your pedigree, your background—those are things you cannot renounce.

I'm sure Martinez will be more than happy that his children's veins will run with Derwent blood to dilute his own.'

Before she could respond, annoyance swept the aquiline cast of his face.

'I had better go and find Juanita. It looks like she is in conversation with a member of the string quartet. Any minute now she will persuade them to play some song she can dance to.'

As he departed Cora narrowed her eyes. 'Good luck to her,' she muttered, and then spun round at the approach of her mother.

Her heart sank at the annoyance in the Duchess's emerald eyes. It belied the mother-of-the-bride smile on her coral-pink lips.

'Did you upset Don Carlos?' she demanded in a low tone. 'I *told* you, Cora—this wedding is designed to show Prince Frederick and the whole Lycander family the worth of the Derwents, and that our connection with the Duque de Aiza counterweights our new *association*—' the word dripped contempt '—with Rafael Martinez. So you need to charm Don Carlos—or at least not alienate him.'

'I...'

The icy light of disappointment in her mother's eyes had the age-old effect of turning Cora's insides to a mush of misery and blanking her brain. *Think of the future, Cora.* Soon her marriage would be over and she would hand over a considerable sum of money to her parents. Then her mother's eyes would hold warmth and approval.

For once the fantasy that soothed her didn't work its usual magic.

'Is everything all right?'

Ah, that would explain it—her senses had clearly been distracted by the approach of Rafael. The deep timbre of his voice warmed her skin and brought back a sudden vivid image of their clinch.

'Everything is fine,' the Duchess averred. 'Just a little mother-daughter chat.' Her gaze swept the room. 'Excuse me. I must find Kaitlin.'

For another 'mother-daughter chat', no doubt. Prince Frederick was surrounded by a bevy of beauties and Kaitlin was conspicuous only by her absence.

Rafael's expression was unreadable—although his gaze was intense, as if he weighed her soul—and she summoned yet another smile. 'We'd better circulate.'

Not that it mattered now. The knot was tied and this reception was now geared to showcase Kaitlin and promote her ascent to royalty. Hence the profusion of flowers that garlanded the marquee, the beautiful centrepieces that decked the snowy-white linen tablecloths. Hence the colour scheme picked to complement the Titian of Kaitlin's hair, the seating arrangements that somehow sidelined the bride and groom and shone a spotlight on the chief bridesmaid, inviting Prince Frederick to observe Kaitlin's eminent suitability as a Lycander bride.

The speeches were met with laughter, and perhaps it was only Cora who noted the imbalance of her father's speech, tipped towards Kaitlin, his older daughter by five minutes. Most of the anecdotes he recalled centred round Kaitlin, with the occasional 'and Cora' tacked on. The rest of them were of necessity pure fallacy, seeing as in truth her parents had avoided Cora's company whenever possible.

As for the message the Duke read from Gabriel, that wished his little sister 'all the best' and expressed his deep sorrow that he couldn't attend her nuptials...as she listened Cora knew it was all hooey. True, she and Gabriel weren't close—her brother had always been distant—but the message smacked of something her parents would concoct.

Perhaps Gabriel had asked them to do it because he disapproved of her marriage. But that didn't sound like him either. Anxiety whispered, only to be dismissed—Gabriel was too assured, too handsome, too golden to be in trouble.

Now Ethan had taken the stage, and as best man he did a gallant job—despite Cora's conviction that the man had his own doubts. On the Cavershams' return from Paris she and Rafael had announced their engagement, and she had witnessed first-hand the surprise on the couple's faces. Some of their surprise had no doubt been due to the revelation that Cora was a member of the aristocracy, but she suspected most of it was down to utter bafflement at the romantic whirlwind scenario.

True, their perplexity had been succeeded by congratulations, champagne, and the assurance that Cora was free to leave work with no hard feelings whatsoever and would be welcome back any time, but Cora knew Ethan and Ruby held reservations as to the validity of their sudden engagement. Guilt touched her that she had avoided all Ruby's attempts to make contact—too worried that she would break down and confess the truth to this woman she liked so much. Then the proverbial fat and fire would be conjoined—Ruby would march up to Rafael and pull the whole deal apart.

And she didn't want that.

The realisation shocked her in its intensity. Despite the falseness of this whole wedding, despite her mortification, she didn't want to cancel the deal. Because she needed the money. Nothing to do with the growing knowledge that this deal meant more than business to Rafael.

Because as the day spun out into evening she knew that there was no way a man like Rafael would go through all this without some stronger motivation than business.

'Now the dancing shall begin. Will the bride and groom take the floor?'

The strains of a familiar melody started.

'I didn't choose this.' Indignation strummed inside her.

'No. I did. I thought it suited our supposed courtship.'

And it did—its melody haunted the air with the tale of a whirlwind love and a happy-ever-after. Words of happiness and joy and hopes of a bright new start in life.

The sheer hypocrisy suddenly made her rage inside that he had chosen it in cold blood. The rage a relief, because it carried her to the dance floor in front of the sea of watchers. Its fire blocked out the sheer knee-trembling proximity of him—until the scent of him infused the air around them and pulled her back willy-nilly to *that night*. Until his hands spanned her waist as he pulled her close and she rested her check against the breadth of his chest. Until for a heartbeat she allowed herself to relax, to float on a dream where this was true—where the lyrics echoed their feelings.

Stop it. This is a pretence.

The song was fake, the wedding was false, and if she remained plastered all over him he would think she wanted a replay of their kiss and more. She tensed against him, straightened up and kept the fake smile in place.

Smiles and platitudes—she was awash on an ocean of them as the evening progressed. Champagne flowed, more nibbles appeared—miniature fish and chips, mini bangers in dollops of mash, tiny exquisite tartlets—and her head whirled. Then finally, when she thought her face might disintegrate under the weight of her smile, when her tongue cleaved to the roof of her mouth and tasted the coating of platitudes, it was time to leave.

Kaitlin extracted her and bore her away to change into her going-away dress—a trouser suit that was just a touch the wrong shade of pink for her. Not that she cared—her need to flee was too urgent. Until she clocked the stress on her sister's face under the smile.

'Kait, what's wrong?'

'Just don't throw the bouquet to me. Please, sis.'

'But…' But the Duchess had been very specific in her instructions and… And *what*? If Kaitlin didn't want the bouquet would it be so bad not to chuck it at her? Yes, Cora would face her mother's wrath and, yes, she would disappoint her parents yet again.

She could almost hear the Duchess's voice so clearly. *We should have known Cora wouldn't be able to manage something even as simple as that.* But it would be one more barb amongst many, and soon all those barbs would be wiped out by approval, once she handed the money over. Plus this was her *sister.*

'OK. Consider it done.'

'Thank you. Truly.'

So when it came to it Cora aimed the bouquet as far away from Kaitlin as possible and turned to see it fall into the grasp of Juanita, who looked absolutely horrified and batted it away.

Cora gave a small chuckle.

'Why is that funny?' Rafael's low voice was surprisingly intense.

'Don Carlos wants to marry Juanita off and she's having none of it.'

There was a portent to the following silence, and when she turned Rafael's haunted expression sent a hum of concern through her.

'What's wrong? Do you know Juanita?' she asked.

'Nothing and no.' His voice was brusque. 'Let's get the last bit of this charade over with and get out of here.'

It was only then that it occurred to Cora that they were about to embark on their honeymoon. The idea was enough to send her hurtling back to the dance floor—smile in place, platitudes at the ready.

CHAPTER NINE

RAFAEL LOOKED AROUND the supposed honeymoon suite of the country hotel and frowned in consternation as the shabbiness of its décor permeated the cloud of confused thoughts that fuzzed his brain.

Of course he had known about Alvaro and Juanita, but he had written them off, blocked them out, never considered them as real people. His whole focus was on Don Carlos and revenge. But now he'd met Juanita and emotion twisted his gut at the idea of Don Carlos marrying her off.

Yet his surroundings were impossible to ignore. The lobby had been a precursor of things to come, with its peeling wallpaper and faint smell of must and damp. As for this honeymoon suite—its sheer dowdiness brought irritation and confirmed the disquiet that the wedding had perpetrated within him. Because there had been a vibe about the day that made his skin prickle, and this shunt into a honeymoon that smacked of being 'good enough for the likes of you' cemented the icing on the proverbial wedding cake.

The champagne was warm, the flowers drooped and his frown deepened as he swept the withered petals off the dresser.

'Why did you choose here?' he asked as Cora emerged from the bathroom, where she'd vanished the second they had arrived.

All signs of Cora the bride had been eradicated—her hair hung loose round her face in damp tendrils, her face held not so much as a vestige of make-up, and the pink trouser ensemble had been replaced by jeans and an over-sized sweatshirt with 'Dogs Rule' on it in faded letters.

'I didn't choose it. Veronica, my parents' PA, organised it.'

Cora's voice was clipped with exhaustion, and for a second compassion touched his chest as he took in the smudges under her eyes. It was a compassion he shrugged off—this was a woman who was revolted by his touch, who was in this for the money.

'The owners offered it for free in return for a bit of publicity.'

'I can only hope they didn't specify what sort of publicity. This is a joke.'

A sigh escaped her as she sank gingerly onto a sagging chair. 'Does it matter? This is a fake honeymoon. You've got what you wanted—a wedding that Don Carlos and the world believe to be real.'

'Yes. But I need Don Carlos to continue to believe in our marriage, and this is *not* a realistic honeymoon desti-nation. You should have realised that.'

'*You* could have checked it out—I'm sure Veronica kept you informed.'

'Yes, she did. Right from the morning after you ran out on me, when she emailed to introduce herself. She told me that she was the Derwent PA and you had asked her to keep me up to date with the wedding preparations be-cause you thought it would be *romantic* for us not to be in touch directly until "the big day". Veronica told me that she had arranged a luxury hotel in the beautiful depths of the English countryside for our honeymoon and that you had approved it.'

A flush tinted her cheeks. 'OK. So I should have

checked it. But to be honest I didn't really care. And I *didn't* run out on you.'

Was she for real?

'What would you call it? You left at speed, in the middle of the night. I was worried about you.'

'You were worried about our charade being blown. I was careful. I got a cab to the train station and I lay low until the first train home. I don't get what you're so mad about.'

There was little point in denying he was angry. The way he was pacing the room and yelling was a bit of a giveaway. Hauling in a calming breath, he halted. 'I may not be the King of Relationships but I don't tend to flee the scene after the event.'

'Well, bully for you.' Rising to her feet, she slammed her hands on the curves of her hips. 'I was embarrassed—OK?'

'I got that.' *Loud and clear.* 'I got it that you felt sullied by slumming it with a commoner like me.'

'Sullied?' For a second confusion reigned supreme on her face, and then she rocked backwards as if in shock.

His jaw jabbed with tension. *Keep calm.* 'By someone of my lowly birth. Isn't that what Don Carlos said to you?'

'You...you think that I...agree with Don Carlos? You think that I feel ashamed of kissing you because of your background? How *dare* you believe that of me? If you overheard my conversation with Don Carlos then you must have heard me defend you and refute his ideas.'

'I did—and I applauded your role-playing skills.'

'Well, you wasted your appreciation. I meant every word I said. I *don't* hold my title in reverence and I *do* admire your achievements. That is the truth. As for that night—I do not believe I was "sullied" in any way at all.'

She took another step forward; her gaze was fearless and open as their eyes met and suddenly he was all too aware of her proximity, the fresh smell of soap and shampoo and pure Cora. Warmth touched him that she had defended him—he couldn't remember the last time anyone had. His head whirled and he forced himself to focus—words were just words...not proof of anything. His mother had placed blind, foolish trust in words and love, and it had made her weak and vulnerable and led to her ruin.

'Then why did you run like that? What were you embarrassed about?'

All of a sudden the anger melted from her face and her gaze skittered away from him as she shifted from one bare foot to another.

'Look, let's just forget it. It's over and done with.'

'No. Clearly there is some misconception here and I want to clear it up.'

If there was anything worse than secrets it was misconceptions. Throughout his childhood he'd been fed a diet of fallacy and it had left him spinning in a quagmire of confusion. One minute his mother would tell him his father's identity 'didn't matter', the next day she'd tell him his father had been a soldier, the next month a diplomat, and so on and so forth. The only constant had been her dreamy-eyed look—and the description of the love they had shared, her conviction that one day he'd find her.

He shook the memories off and stepped towards Cora. 'We need to sort this out. I don't deal well with misread situations.'

She hesitated, and then huffed out a sigh that spelled resignation. 'Fine. I can't bear for you to believe that I am tainted by Don Carlos's ideas. I felt mortified by my behaviour, but not for the reasons you think.' She glanced down, as if to gain courage from the shabby carpet, before straightening up. 'You said it yourself. The reason you asked *me* to marry you, rather than someone like Kaitlin, was because you weren't attracted to me.'

'I did say that, but—'

'Then you felt sorry for me, and I threw myself at you, and you were rightly horrified—'

'Whoa! Hold it right there. Pity was *not* at the party.'

'Tchaa.'

It was amazing how much scoff she put into the noise.

'Look, I have as much self-esteem as the next person.'

A statement he doubted was true.

'But I *know* the type of woman you are usually attracted to and I am not in their league.'

'There is no "league". I agree, you are different from the women I usually date, but that is *zip* to do with attraction. I date women who want the same things I want from an association. You don't fit that criteria—you want a happy-ever-after with Joe Average.' *All the more reason he should never have kissed her.* 'Plus, I will not let attraction blur our marriage lines—our marriage is a business deal. Nothing more. But the attraction was real and you have no reason to be embarrassed by your behaviour.'

Her head dipped in acknowledgement but he couldn't shake the idea that she hadn't fully bought into his words. His eyes assessed her expression, wondered what could have knocked her self-esteem so badly. The urge to reassure her washed over him. *Enough.* It had been the urge to reassure her that had landed them in this mess of a conversation in the first place.

'Thank you,' she murmured. 'Now, I'm going to turn in.' Her lips twisted in a small grimace. 'Would you prefer the bedroom? I'm quite happy to have the sofa.'

They both contemplated the lumpy, seen-better-days excuse for a sofa.

Rafael sighed. 'I'll be fine out here.' No one could accuse Rafael Martinez of being unchivalrous.

Cora opened her eyes and decided to abandon any idea of sleep as frivolous. The mattress was way past its use-by date, but she couldn't blame its state for the scratchy feel of her tired eyes. How could she sleep when confusion fuzzed her brain?

The conversation with Rafael had not been the talk she'd expected, and had triggered a conflict of emotions inside her. A dangerous temptation to believe the attraction was real alongside an anger and a funny little ache in her heart at his belief that she'd thought she'd lowered herself by kissing him.

The drumming of rain against the window distracted her and she sighed as she clambered out of bed. English spring at its best—and yet in truth the weather suited her mood, and the drab surroundings and grey vista illustrated the fact that her use to her parents was over. The wedding had been for Kaitlin's benefit and now Cora had been shuffled off-stage and returned to shabby storage.

But not for long—once this marriage was over she would repay her debt and regain her life. So she would not stew in self-pity. Time for a shower and then she would while the day away with a book, avoiding any more conversation with Rafael. A business marriage did *not* require chit-chat.

Fifteen minutes later she pushed the bedroom door open, entered the adjoining living area and paused. Rafael sat at the flimsy wooden table, laptop open in front of him, his dark hair shower-damp, presumably post-visit to the hotel gym, dressed in a long-sleeved grey tee and jeans. *Be still, her beating heart.*

'Good morning.'

He looked up and the frown on his face made her prickle her with foreboding.

'Morning. We have a problem.'

'What sort of problem?'

'This.' Rising, he gestured to his laptop. 'You'd better read these articles on our wedding.'

Bride is pretty, groom is gorgeous, but maid of honour steals the limelight and the eye of Prince Charming!

There can be no doubt that Lady Kaitlin Derwent stole the show from her less well known sister. Though the bride's dress was lavish frilly froth, as ever Kaitlin showed that the 'It' factor cannot be bought, and her simple charm and elegance bewitched Prince Frederick of Lycander...

It was one article of many. Cora scanned a few more headlines: *Kaitlin Derwent rocks it while her sister rolls to second place... Outclassed bride still enjoys celebrations...*

She pushed the computer away. It shouldn't hurt but it did, and each comparison was a jab at an age-old wound. But pride allowed her to shrug.

'It's no big deal. No one has said they don't believe in our relationship.'

His eyes narrowed. 'It's a big deal to me.'

Of course it was. Rafael Martinez would not like to be portrayed as a man who had won the booby prize.

'I don't like the idea of people reading this any more than I like this ridiculous choice of a honeymoon venue.' His strides ate up the worn, faded carpet. 'I'm going to do something about it.'

'No!' Consternation overtook hurt. 'You can't.' Her parents would have an indigo fit if their careful plots and manoeuvres were impeded.

'Yes, I can. This *matters*. I will not have my wife reduced to a second-class bride and do nothing.'

It really did matter to him. He was looking at her, but she had a feeling he was seeing something or someone from his past. More to the point, Rafael had *paid* for the wedding. Guilt touched her and she clenched her nails into her palms—she owed him the truth. However hard her tummy twisted at the thought, she couldn't hide behind a wall of lies.

'Rafael. I need to tell you something. The wedding… Kaitlin upstaging me—it was deliberate.'

There was a long moment of silence. 'Explain.'

'My parents saw the wedding as a chance to promote a marriage between Kaitlin and Prince Frederick. The idea was to present Kaitlin as the perfect candidate for royalty, and if that meant sidelining the bride then so be it.'

No need to supply Rafael with the exact words. *'Kaitlin outclasses you anyway, Cora—we may as well take advantage of it.'*

'It wasn't a big deal—they just designed the wedding to impress Frederick and show off Kaitlin.'

They had chosen Cora a dress she'd loathed—all frills and fuss so that Kaitlin's classic beauty would stand out—picked a colour scheme that suited Kaitlin, made sure the photographer knew the score, and Bob was your uncle… or Frederick was your son-in-law.

'At your expense?'

'Yes. But it really doesn't matter. It wasn't a real wedding, and I knew a wedding designed to impress the House of Lycander would also impress Don Carlos.'

'So you don't mind this?' He gestured at the computer.

'No. I have long since accepted that Kaitlin is more beautiful than I am, as well as more…more *everything*. The point is no matter what dress I wore Kaitlin's natural grace and beauty would have put me in the shade. So why not let some good come of it? It doesn't bother me.'

Because she wouldn't let it—she had come to terms and made her peace with her family's dynamic.

'I'm not sure I believe that. Comments like this are hurtful—and besides, Kaitlin isn't *"more everything"* than you. Your appearance was deliberately sabotaged by your parents. I don't see how you *can* be OK with it. Either way—I'm not. Regardless of your parents' agenda I will *not* let you be sidelined, nor allow your parents to display their true belief as to my worth. Or yours.'

There was a hint of compassion in his voice that made her wince; she could not bear to be an object of pity yet again.

'Well, you'd better believe it. I am completely on board with their plan and those articles do *not* bother me.'

CHAPTER TEN

RAFAEL LOOKED AT CORA, seated at the rickety table, her turquoise eyes narrowed as she gazed at him. For a moment curiosity displaced the cold burn of anger at the Derwents' behaviour. His mother had been a tragic victim of aristocratic arrogance and he didn't like the echo of that in the here and now. But *why* was Cora content to accept these malicious comments in the press? *Why* had she agreed to a deliberate portrayal of herself as second best?

'OK.' He pulled out a chair and sat down opposite her. 'Convince me.'

Cora scrunched her forehead as if in internal debate, placed her elbows on the table and rested her chin on her cupped hands.

'I don't mind the headlines and I didn't mind the wedding because I've accepted reality. For years I strove to be more like Kaitlin—more beautiful, more clever, more serene, more graceful, more—' She broke off. 'More everything, I guess.'

'Why not be happy being you?'

'That's easy to say, but when your twin sister represents perfection that's what you aspire to, right? Kaitlin was immensely popular, cool and beautiful. People were only interested in me as a gateway to her.'

'That must have been tough.'

Her eyes narrowed. 'I am not looking for sympathy—I

just want to explain how I *am* perfectly OK with the situation.'

'OK.' He raised a hand. 'No more interruptions.'

'When I was twenty-one I met Rupert. I'd given up on romance because I was fed up with being simply a conduit to Kaitlin or only desired for my title. But I thought Rupert was different. He seemed different—interested in *me* as a person. We spent time together and I fell for him. Big-time. He made me believe it was possible for someone to prefer me to Kaitlin. One night I decided to go to party I knew he'd be at. I dressed up to the nines and decided to bare my soul—and a whole lot else.'

For a moment Rafael could almost see her, standing on the edge of the party, hair loose, giving a quick swipe of her hand to the skirt of her dress to smooth it, her turquoise eyes wide and oh, so vulnerable.

'What happened?'

'I did my throwing myself at him routine and he... Well, he rejected me. Poor man was mortified—he was lovely and kind, but he explained that it was Kaitlin he loved. He knew he didn't have a chance with her, and he wasn't using me to get to her, but being with me made him feel closer to her. I felt like such a fool.'

Of course she had. Rafael's gut twisted at her humiliation. 'I'm sor—'

'No interruptions,' she reminded him. 'I saw that Rupert had done me a favour. He told me that I was—and I quote— "a pale imitation of Kaitlin...a shadow." And I realised he was right. That no matter what I did, how I dressed, how hard I studied, how much I tried, I would never be on a par with Kaitlin. That's when I came to terms with it—decided to accept that I am who I am and that is OK. That's why things like those headlines don't matter any more.'

It all made sense—Cora had given up trying to be like

her sister. Which was great. Except he could spot the flaw. She'd given up full-stop—still believed she was inferior to Kaitlin, a pale shadow of her twin. The only difference was that she'd decided to accept it. That was why she'd rejected the gold dress he'd bought her to wear for dinner with her family, why she wore clothes that muted her, worked at a job that didn't inspire her. Cora had built herself protective armour—told herself that if she didn't try she wouldn't feel a failure.

She frowned. 'What are you thinking?'

'I'm thinking that Rupert was wrong. You aren't a pale shadow of Kaitlin. You are you, and you need to work out who Cora Derwent is and feel good about it.'

He wasn't sure why she felt as she did, but sensed that Rupert had been the tip of the iceberg—the culmination of a stream of events that had knocked her self-esteem out of the ball park and way beyond.

'What is *that* supposed to mean?' Indignation sparked in the turquoise of her eyes. 'I know exactly who I am and I am happy with that person. *Very* happy. That was the whole point of me telling you all that. To prove it.'

'I...' Rafael pressed his lips together.

Best to leave well alone—Cora believed she had it all sorted and maybe she did. Maybe he was reading way more into the situation than there was on the page. Lady Cora Derwent had money, family, and was quite capable of living her own life without his input. They were *business* partners and it was business he needed to consider now.

So... 'Good,' he said. 'I'm glad you're OK with this mess. But I'm not, and if you think we're going to languish here in this godforsaken hotel you can think again.'

'What are we going to do?'

'We are going to honeymoon in style and make sure the press knows about it. You'll have to swallow your principles and board another private jet.'

'To where?'

'To Granada.'

It made sense for them to be in Spain, to make a bit of a splash in the Spanish press...remind Don Carlos of his existence.

A few hours later Cora looked around the interior of the private jet and felt a sense of *déjà-vu* descend. And yet there was a difference to this trip. This time she and Rafael were man and wife—an outcome she would never have foretold in a million years a few weeks before.

A glance at him now showed a man at ease as he leafed through a magazine. Yet over the past few hours he had arranged this trip with lightning speed and an assurance Cora could only envy—maybe it was because Rafael Martinez knew exactly who he was and what he wanted and felt *excellent* about it.

Her thoughts went back to his words. *'You need to work out who Cora Derwent is and feel good about it.'*

That was exactly what she'd done, for goodness' sake. Accepted who she was and got on with her life. Decided that as she could never be Kaitlin she would win her parents' love via a different route—proving her use to them. That was a good thing, right? So there was no need to let Rafael's words niggle at her like this. The man had known her a scant few weeks—his opinion was hardly valid.

But still his words haunted her—he'd uttered them so thoughtfully, as if he knew he was right. As if he could see something she couldn't.

So when he glanced up her mouth opened and she said, 'Do you really think that I don't know who I am?'

Opposite her Rafael blinked, but didn't miss a beat. 'I think you have been so busy comparing yourself to Kaitlin you don't realise your own assets—your looks, your abilities, your potential.'

There was no judgement in that simple statement.

'In what way?'

He shrugged. 'Over the past weeks you've told me what you want from life. To be happy. To be ordinary. To live happily ever after with Joe Average. To work with dogs. Yet you aren't doing *any* of those things.'

'It's not that easy.'

'Yes, it is.' He tipped his palms in the air. 'Do it. Set up Derwent's Dogs. Advertise and start walking dogs. Set up a kennel. You might meet Joe A or you might end up with franchises all over the world. You can do anything you want to. Or you can at least try.'

His words seemed to emphasise the differences between them—Rafael thought universally *big*. How boring she must seem to him—pedestrian, almost. 'That's not my choice. I'm not like you—I want *ordinary*, remember?'

'Then start small and stay small. Or study to be a vet. The possibilities are endless. But whatever you do make sure it's what you *want* to do. You aren't a pale imitation of Kaitlin and you don't have to live in her shadow. It's *your* life. Live it.'

The words were said with an intensity that sent a shiver to her very soul, gave her the belief that he meant every one.

But words were easy and, whilst she deemed his sincerity to be real, she needed to hang on to reality. That reality dictated family obligation and the importance of *her* goal. Rafael might have hidden depths, but right now they had been thrown together by a business deal. Within days she would pall for him, and once this marriage was over he would forget her within minutes and move on. So she needed to hold on to the rules that governed her lifestyle and not be beguiled by his.

'I do plan to live it. I know what I want from life.' Her

parents' love and approval…the chance to prove she was a true Derwent.

Before he could reply his phone rang, and within seconds there was an exchange of dialogue, the words uttered in rapid-fire Spanish. Could it be Don Carlos? Already? The thought gave her pause—hope mixed with an inexplicable trickle of disappointment. At the thought of missing out on Granada, *obviously*.

'Is everything OK?' she asked once he'd ended the conversation.

'That was a Spanish gossip magazine reporter I left a message for earlier—Cristina Herrera. She's agreed to meet us tomorrow for a honeymoon interview. That should help make it clear that our honeymoon is not a second-class event. I know you don't like the limelight, but I think this is important. With a bit of luck Don Carlos may even read it.'

'No problem.' Cora tried to inject confidence into her voice. In truth the whole idea left her frozen, but she could see his point of view. 'I faked an entire wedding—this will be a doddle.'

Only it didn't feel that way—this time the spotlight would be focused solely on her and Rafael. No Kaitlin, no Duke and Duchess, and no array of glittering celebrities for the paps to focus on. Just her. A frisson of nerves rippled through her.

'I'll even let them dress me up so I look a bit more Kaitlinesque.'

What? Where had that come from?

Rafael looked as though he were wondering the same thing. Cora could almost see his mental eye-roll.

'That's not what you need to do at all. You don't *need* to look "Kaitlinesque". You need to look *Cora*-esque. Wear whatever makes you feel good without comparing yourself to Kaitlin.'

'No problem. Easy-peasy.' Had she really said that? 'I'll stick to my own wardrobe, then.'

To her own irritation she could hear the mixture of defiance and defensiveness in her voice. Which was mad. There was nothing to defy *or* defend. Surely she could find something in her suitcase that would make her feel good? Yet as she mentally reviewed the medley of dark, oversized garments that made up her wardrobe doubts began to creep in. This was ridiculous—it didn't *matter* what she wore. Clothes were just bits of material, necessary to maintain decency and keep you warm.

Her navy blue sundress would be fine. An image of the dress floated to the forefront of her mind. Loose-fitting. Buttoned-up neck. Puffy sleeves. Now the doubts began to stockpile. Had she *really* chosen her clothes to deliberately mask any hint of femininity? Had she *actually* decided to become invisible rather than a pale shadow of Kaitlin?

Suddenly aware of the slightly sardonic gleam in Rafael's eyes, she narrowed her own.

'Easy-peasy, lemon-squeezy,' she stated as she picked up a magazine.

Enough. These thoughts were a product of being around someone like Rafael Martinez, with his Hollywood looks and charisma and his larger than life persona. She could only hope this honeymoon was as short-lived as possible.

CHAPTER ELEVEN

RAFAEL SCOOPED COFFEE into the cafetière and gazed out of the wooden-framed kitchen window. The early-morning Spanish sunshine shed its dappled rays on the pavement as he inhaled the familiar aroma of Granada—a heady mix of exotic spice mingled with the glorious smell of orange blossom and a waft of tea leaves.

'Good morning.'

He turned at the sound of Cora's soft voice and leant against the marble-topped counter. 'Morning...' Her glorious hair was piled on top of her head and a few tendrils fell loose round her face; her expression was a mix of uncertainty and a flicker of defiance, as if she was daring him to comment.

Presumably on her choice of dress...Rafael schooled his features to remain neutral at the sight of the sheer staidness of the navy blue sundress and swallowed a sigh. How Cora dressed was irrelevant—if that was what made her feel good, so be it. Yet the idea that she lived her life in her sister's shadow sent a twinge of frustration through him.

Life really was too short—he knew that. His mother's final months had been weighted with regret that she had lived a decade in the shadow cast by his father's betrayal. That knowledge was woven into the fabric of his identity— a reminder as to why he and Cora were in this apartment in

Granada. Their purpose was to fake a honeymoon—there was no item on the agenda that declared a need to help Lady Cora Derwent with her emotional baggage. Heaven knew that was hardly his forte, and yet for reasons he couldn't fathom he wanted to make her see herself as she truly was.

'The reporter will be here in an hour. We'd best get ready.'

'I *am* ready.' Shoulders back, she narrowed her eyes. 'You told me to dress in a Cora-esque fashion. This is it.'

'I meant we need to move our clothes and so on into the same bedroom, just in case she does a journalistic sneak peek whilst pretending to use the bathroom.'

Cora stilled, an expression of pain sweeping her features, and he blinked. He filtered his words on a rerun but was none the wiser.

'I'm not suggesting you actually move in to my bedroom,' he clarified. And then wished he hadn't as, unbidden, the idea of sharing a bed and a whole lot more with her sent a reel of images through his brain. The memory of her lips against his…the soft, sweet passion of their kiss…the texture of her skin beneath his fingers…the press of her body against his…

Whoa. Don't go there.

'I understand that.' Her voice low, with a huskiness that sent his senses into overdrive. 'Let's get a move on.'

Half an hour later, as she smoothed the duvet on her bed, he glanced round to ensure there was no stray evidence of her occupancy. 'Looks good,' he said, just as the doorbell chimed. 'You ready?'

'As I'll ever be.'

Rafael frowned as her lips turned up into the smile he recognised as wholly fake. His mind whirred—no reporter worth their salt would be taken in. Not in a private interview. However well he and Cora had rehearsed their words.

The wild idea of kissing her entered his head—he knew

that would ignite a spark and summon a genuine smile to their faces. But that way spelt danger, and the risk of blurring a line he would not allow himself even to smudge.

Instead he asked, 'What do you feed an invisible cat?'

The smile dropped from her lips as her forehead scrunched into lines of confusion. 'Huh?'

'It's a joke.'

'You're telling me a joke *now*?'

'Yup. Come on—this one is hilarious.' Jokes had been one of the few things that had made his mother laugh, and so as a child he had spent hours conning every joke book he could lay his hands on.

'Um…I don't know.'

'Evaporated milk.'

Cora stared at him, turquoise eyes wide with disbelief, and then a gurgle of laughter fell from her lips. 'That is the most ridiculous joke I've ever heard.'

'Try this one. What does a philosophical dolphin think about?'

'No idea.'

'Have I got a porpoise?'

To his own surprise the joke he had thought long since forgotten brought a smile to his own lips as she shook her head in mock sorrow. 'Where on earth did you get those from?'

'It doesn't matter.' And it didn't—right now the important thing was that Cora looked genuinely more relaxed and happy, in time for the reporter. 'There are plenty more where they came from, though.'

'I can't wait.'

'OK. Now, let's let Cristina in.'

'Let's do it.'

'So…' Cristina began, once she was seated on the leather sofa in the lounge. 'First, thank you for seeing me—I was surprised, given it's the first day of your honeymoon.'

Rafael smiled. 'It wasn't part of our honeymoon plan, but after the press coverage of our wedding I wanted to make it very clear to all those readers out there that I don't in any way feel I got the "second-best" sister. I want the world to know that Cora Derwent is the woman I…the woman for me.'

His lips were unable to use the word *love* even in pretence, and he could only hope Cristina hadn't clocked his infinitesimal stumble. Love was a word to be eschewed and dreaded; it led the way to allowing someone else power over you.

'And how do *you* feel about the comments on your wedding?' Cristina asked as she turned to Cora.

Cora smoothed the blue cotton of her sundress down. 'To be honest, Cristina, they bothered Rafael more than me. I had a wonderful day because I married Rafael— nothing can take away from that memory. Now I want to get on with our life, beginning with this wonderful surprise honeymoon. I have always wanted to see Granada and now I can.'

'So that's your plan whilst you're here—to soak up the sights?'

'Absolutely,' Rafael interjected. 'I am looking forward to sharing Granada with Cora. The Basilica de San Juan de Dios—I'm sure you'll agree the altar of gold needs to be seen to be believed. And I'd also like to take Cora to the Alhambra de Granada…'

'How does that sound to you, Cora?'

'Wonderful. Although actually there is one other thing I'd like to do whilst I'm here, though I haven't had a chance to discuss this with Rafael yet.'

Rafael blinked. OK—Cora had clearly decided to deviate from the script.

She leant forward a little and animation illuminated her features. 'I'm hoping to look up a friend of mine—Sally

Anne Gregory. Sally Anne set up a dog rescue charity here in Granada a couple of years ago and I took on one of her first rescues. A gorgeous Spanish Shepherd dog called Prue. But there are still a horrendous number of abandoned dogs here. A lot of puppies bought and then, when they grow bigger, simply left somewhere so they roam the streets, scavenge from bins and sleep in doorways and shop fronts. It's incredibly sad—if you could see some of these animals…it's criminal.'

Rafael could hear the passion and compassion in her voice, sense how much she cared from the tilt of her body and the jut of her chin, and it touched him.

'Anyway, now that I'm here I would like to meet Sally Anne and let her know in person how much I admire what she's doing. Oh, and show her loads of photos of Prue.'

'Do you have any other dogs?'

'Just one. Another rescue called Poppy. I'd love more, but it's not practical.'

'After the honeymoon presumably you'll bring your dogs to live with you? Will that be here or in London?'

'Um…I… We…'

Next to him Cora stiffened and he could almost see Cristina's reporter antennae twitch.

Rafael's mind whirred. 'At the moment Cora and I are in discussions about the best place for us to live. But wherever we go of course Prue and Poppy will be with us.'

Rising to his feet, he decided to head off any conversation about the intricacies of their future. After all it would be a waste of breath, because there would be no cosy, white picket fence future and he had no wish to envisage any such nightmare. He doubted his ability to pretend with even a modicum of conviction.

'Now, would you like a tour and a few quick photographs?'

Once the reporter had left Cora turned to him and

tipped her palms in the air. 'Sorry. I didn't mean to mention the dogs or Sally Anne. It just suddenly occurred to me what great publicity it would be for Sally Anne and I blurted it out. I know it threw us into the deep end and I shouldn't have done it, but...'

'Whoa. It's OK, Cora. No harm, no foul.'

'Really?'

'Really. Could even be a good tactic—the amount you care about the plight of those dogs was obvious and *real*. It was very Cora Derwent and a far cry from Kaitlin. Cristina's article will be about *you*—and that was the aim. Plus, it took the focus off our romance which was a relief—I found it hard to pretend to believe in happy-ever-after.'

After all he knew it didn't exist, and he knew the folly of believing that it did.

Cora shook her head. 'But there's proof. There are gazillions of happily married couples in the world.'

'There are lots of *married* couples in the world,' he corrected.

'Don't you think that's a bit cynical?'

'No. Think about it. How many of those couples stay together for the children, or for tax reasons, or because they're scared to be alone? How many of them set aside their dreams for the sake of their marriage?'

Cora lifted her hands as if she wanted to cover her ears, and then dropped them to her sides. 'Even if some of that is true there are lots of people out there who stay together because they love each other.'

'Maybe. But love can cause untold hurt. Why take the risk?'

'Because you trust the other person.'

'Trust?' It wasn't possible for him to put sufficient scorn into the word. 'Trust is pointless. Because people can deceive you. Or, worse, you can deceive yourself.' Her wince showed he'd hit home. 'Do you *really* believe it's possible to place absolute trust in someone else?'

'I…I don't know.'

'Exactly. So why take the risk? When the only benefit you'd get is the doubtful possibility of a happy*ish* marriage. And you'd risk the very distinct probability of the dwindling and disappearance of love. The near certainty of loss. There is no such thing as a happy-ever-after. Life dictates that there must be some unhappiness.'

'Enough, already. I get your point, and I'm not sure I can logically combat any of your arguments, but I think it's a risk worth taking with the right person.'

Rafael shrugged. 'Well, I hope one day you find that person.' The average, ordinary guy she craved. For some reason the idea of the mythical Joe Average sent a skitter of irritation down his nerves. 'But right now how about we go explore Granada? I have tickets for the Alhambra.'

Cora soaked in the ambience of Granada. The hustle and bustle, the glorious smells, the sheer vibrancy seeped into her bones. The stress of the wedding and her interview nerves faded away, impossible to maintain as Rafael spoke about Granada, his love of the place clear in his every deep-timbred word, his knowledge of its history impressive.

She listened spellbound to the story of how Granada had risen over the centuries to become one of the most prosperous medieval cities in Europe, until the fifteenth century when civil and religious wars devastated the countryside and finally resulted in the siege of Granada itself.

'Followed by the triumphant entry of Isabel and Fernando, the conquering Catholic Monarchs, who entered the city garbed in ceremonial Muslim dress.'

'Tell me more.'

Rafael shook his head. 'Later. You need to look around, see the Granada of today.'

He was right, and there was so much to take in. Music permeated the air, and the clack of maracas as street dancers torqued and swayed mingled with the sound of an accordion and the quick-fire riff of spoken Spanish. As for the food—Cora couldn't decide what she craved most as she looked at the luscious fruits on display.

'They smell like *real* strawberries,' she stated.

'As opposed to imaginary ones?'

His smile made her toes tingle. 'Ha-ha! I mean they smell like strawberries should smell, but supermarket ones never do. Even the pineapples look more...pineapply.'

'It's a shame it's not autumn—you'd love the seasonal fruit then. There's *cherimoya*, also known as a custard apple, persimmons, quince and *azuifaifa*.'

'What's *azuifaifa*?'

'It looks like an acorn and tastes like an apple. I think the English translation is Chinese date.'

Curiosity surfaced. 'How do you know so much about Spain?'

A rueful smile tipped his lips. 'Have I been boring you?'

'No! You've made Granada past and present come alive for me.' She shrugged. 'I just wondered whether your family lived in Spain and that's why you speak the language and love it so much.'

It was the wrong question to have asked—the relaxed stance of his body morphed into tension and the smile vanished from his lips as if it had never been.

'Something like that.' He glanced at his watch. 'We'd better grab lunch if we want to get to the Alhambra by two.'

His withdrawal was palpable as they walked to a small restaurant. When would she learn to think before she spoke? It had been a stupid question—after all, Rafael had invited no family members at all to the wedding...evidence enough that his family was a topic to avoid.

As they sat outside at a white plastic table, under the shade of a canopy, Cora scanned the menu. But she couldn't focus on the black italics.

'I'm really sorry—I didn't mean to pry. Truly. Your family circumstances are none of my business.'

For a moment she thought he'd simply agree, and she wished *again* that she'd kept her big mouth shut. Why was she so gauche?

'I don't want to make this awkward. I was really enjoying our conversation and I love Granada. I don't want to spoil it with my big mouth.'

He studied her expression for a long moment and then he shrugged. 'It was a fair question. I grew up not knowing who my father was. The one fact I did have was that he was Spanish, so I became an expert on all things Spanish. You could say I was a touch obsessed. Hence my knowledge.' The words were said with a casualness that belied their importance. 'You may as well make the most of it,' he continued. 'I can translate the menu for you.'

Cora hauled in a deep breath. Clearly Rafael did not want to discuss this. He had only imparted the information in a defensive attempt to pretend it was no big deal.

'Better yet, why don't you order for us?' she suggested as a waiter approached.

'Sure.'

Once done, Rafael leant back, and she watched the play of light and shadow cast by the early-afternoon rays dapple his features.

'So what are we having?'

'I've ordered some typical dishes. There's *patatas a lo pobre*, which literally means potatoes of the poor. The potatoes are slowly fried in olive oil with green peppers and onion. And *plato alpujarreño*—you can't come to Granada and not try it. It's dried pork sausage with a fried egg. Then

I thought we'd finish with bread and *queso curado*—I'm not sure how they cure the cheese, but it's a unique taste.'

'That sounds perfect.'

And the food, when it arrived, was incredible. The earthy tastes lingered on her tastebuds as she savoured the spice of the meat and the flavour of the potatoes. But even as she enjoyed each mouthful her mind dwelled on a small, dark-haired Rafael genning up on all things Spanish in order to create some sort of link with a man he'd never known. A man who had given him the colour of his hair and the Mediterranean hue of his skin. A man who had presumably abandoned him.

'Penny for them?' Rafael asked.

Her brain scuttled for a platitude and gave up. 'I'm sorry about your dad. I understand that you don't want to talk about it, but I want you to know that.'

'There is no need to be sorry. I've done fine without him. The only reason I don't want to talk about him is that he isn't worth the time or breath.' He pushed his plate away with a decisive gesture. 'So, if you're finished, let's go to the Alhambra.'

Cora studied his expression and gained zilch—there was a tension to his jaw, but little else to suggest that the topic under discussion was of more importance than the weather. The man quite clearly did not wish for sympathy or comment.

'Let's go,' she said.

As they walked the avenue lined with an ancient canopy of gnarled trees Rafael questioned why on earth he'd mentioned his father at all. It must have been the mix of utter contrition and self-reproach on Cora's face, the sense he'd had that she was used to censure for blurting out something supposedly inappropriate. Still, whatever his reason it had been foolhardy, and he could only be relieved that she had spared him an in-depth analysis.

As if suddenly aware of the silence Cora looked up at him, and her prettiness struck him anew.

'What?' Her hand flew up to her chin. 'Have I got egg yolk on my face?'

'No. I was thinking how pretty you are.'

Her face tinted. 'Really?'

'Really.'

'Um…then, thank you, I guess. I mean—' Breaking off, she grimaced. 'Anyway. Clearly I'm not good with compliments so I'll shut up. Let's talk about the Alhambra instead.'

A good plan—what was wrong with him? Cora might not be good with compliments but he had no business handing them out—they were *business* partners.

Yet a sneaking suspicion crept in that somehow Cora was getting under his skin, and it made said skin prickle with foreboding. The phrase made him think of Ethan's description of falling for Ruby.

'It's hard to explain, mate,' his friend had said. 'One minute I knew I was immune to love, the next somehow Ruby had permeated that immunity and love took seed and grew and flourished.'

Well, that wasn't happening to Rafael—the only apposite thing about Ethan's analogy was the idea that love was a disease—one *he* would not succumb to by so much as one tiny germ.

Time to morph into a tour guide.

'You'll love the Alhambra.'

Part palace, part fort, it was a place of Moorish beauty mixed with Christian influence and splendour that never failed to bring him a measure of awe-filled peace. The glory of the architecture, the sound of the fountains and the rustle of leaves, the noise of the nightingales and the scents of wildflower and myrtle.

'Moorish poets called it "a pearl set in emeralds" because of the colour of the buildings and the surrounding woods.'

As they made their way through the Nasrid palaces he spouted forth information on the Nasrid dynasty. He tried to ignore the funny little tug to his heartstrings at the intent look of awe and wonder on Cora's face as she absorbed the glory of their surroundings.

'It all started with Mohammed ben Al-Hamar, in the thirteenth century, who established a royal residency here. The palaces grew from there. It was Yusuf I and Mohammed V who did most of what we can see today...including this—the Patio de los Leones.'

'Yet even the Nasrid family tree ended, didn't it?' Cora said as they entered the Patio. 'They had to give the Alhambra up.'

'The last "King" of Granada was Boabdil. He negotiated a surrender with Ferdinand and Isabella and was granted a fiefdom. It is said that once he departed Granada he stopped about twelve kilometres from the city, looked back at what he had lost—his heritage in all its splendour—and understandably he sighed. His mother said, "You do well to weep like a woman for what you could not defend like a man."'

Cora gave a small laugh that held more than a hint of bitterness and no mirth whatsoever. 'That may have happened centuries ago, but if my brother lost Derwent Manor now I can imagine my mother saying much the same.'

'At least no one will battle him for the Manor, so he can't really lose it. Unless he decides to pass it on to a heritage trust.'

'He won't. He will do as my parents have—devote his

life to raising enough funds to maintain the Manor. Do whatever it takes to keep the Manor.'

'*Whatever* it takes? What if it was morally wrong?'

The crease of her forehead denoted frustration. 'I don't know where Gabe stands on morals. My parents believe anything is justifiable to keep Derwent Manor in the family's hands, that there is no sacrifice too big, that wrong is right. They believe in the bloodline and in the importance of Derwent property being handed on intact from father to son.'

The same beliefs held by the Duques de Aiza—the belief that had dictated Ramon Aiza's betrayal, his cruel discard of Emma and Rafael.

'What about you? What do *you* believe?'

'I'd like to believe that right and wrong are more important—that individual wants and needs should be taken into account. That if Gabe doesn't want to uphold the Derwent heritage he shouldn't have to. But it's not that easy. I guess the point is a true Derwent would want to uphold the heritage and there is no choice involved—it's a given.'

'Because duty to your heritage is more important than anything else?'

Ramon had presumably felt *his* duty to his bloodline had been more important than his duty to the woman who loved him and his son.

Cora shrugged. 'You feel you have a duty to the people who work on your vineyard, but not to the land itself. You could walk away without a care. Don Carlos…my parents—they feel a connection with the soil and the bricks and mortar, because it has been in their family for centuries. If you passed your vineyard on in a few hundred years it would become Martinez land and your descendants would feel a duty to it.'

For an insane moment the idea held an appeal—an appeal he rejected out of hand. His ethos was to live for the moment, not for centuries ahead. 'Not going to happen. Because I won't be passing the vineyard on to any child.'

Curiosity alongside bafflement sparked in her eyes. 'So you don't have any desire to have kids?'

'I've thought about it. But it doesn't compute. I have no wish to commit to one woman for the rest of my life, but if I had a child I would want to be a proper part of that child's life.'

There was no way he would ever bring a baby into the world knowing he couldn't be there for him or her every single day.

Rafael huffed out a sigh. How did he end up in these conversations with Cora? No other woman would question him on his lifestyle choices. It was probably because they were too busy enjoying all the perks of said lifestyle.

'Anyway, we'd better move on. There's a lot to see.' Definitely time to resume the tour guide role. 'This is the Patio de los Leones.'

He gestured to the centrepiece of the courtyard—a fountain made of twelve lions topped by a dodecagon-shaped basin. Water sparkled as it fell from the mouths of the white marble creatures who symbolised strength, power, and sovereignty.

'It's one of the most important examples of Muslim sculpture—and it's certainly one of the most beautiful and the most scientific. There is a poem by Ibn Zamrak, a four-teenth-century poet, carved on the basin. He describes the fountain something like this. "Melted silver flows through the pearls, which it resembles in its pure dawn beauty."'

Next to him Cora caught her breath as she gazed at the fountain, seemingly oblivious to the crowds of tourists that milled around the floor. 'That's beautiful.'

'It is, but he ends the poem wishing that the peace of God will go with the reader and says *"May your life be*

long and unscathed, multiplying your feasts and torment-
ing your enemies.'"

Cora looked up at him. 'You say that with way too
much feeling. Do you agree that your enemy should be
tormented?'

'Yes.' His answer was unequivocal. After all that was
the whole reason for this marriage deal—a means to torment Don Carlos, Duque de Aiza. Yet the look in her eyes
sent a strange defensive twinge through him. 'I take it
you don't?'

'I think it depends on the circumstances, but I guess
I'm not a great believer in tormenting anyone. I know it
depends on why you're enemies, but surely it's better to
try and sort the situation out rather than escalate it? I suppose it's a bit like facing an aggressive dog: the solution
isn't to be aggressive back.'

At the thought of sorting *anything* out with Don Carlos
he felt black thoughts grounding his feet as Cora moved
away to explore the rest of the courtyard. Yet as he watched
her warmth spread in his chest and dissipated the darkness, chased away the thoughts of revenge.

Suddenly aware of the way his gaze tracked her as she
walked around the marble columns, her features touched
with wonder, no doubt counting the damn things, he
scrubbed a hand down his face. What was wrong with
him? Revenge was exactly what he needed to be focused
on—this honeymoon was merely a necessary interlude
until he could realistically contact Don Carlos. Of course
he wanted Cora to seize the moment and have fun, but that
was a fringe benefit in the true purpose of this marriage.

And he had no intention of forgetting it.

CHAPTER TWELVE

Cora gazed at the contents of the sleek dark wardrobe and tried to decide what to do.

The obvious choice for dinner in a flamenco restaurant was the same dress she had worn when she'd gone out for dinner with Rafael and her family. The problem was she didn't *want* to wear that dress. She wanted to wear the other dress. The one Rafael had given her. The one that had tempted her gaze with its shimmer of gold.

And what sort of message would *that* send out?

Rafael's words echoed in her brain. *'Keep the dress for another occasion, another time when you do feel comfortable in it. Because you will wow the world or the man you wear it for.'*

Just flipping great. So now she wanted to *wow* Rafael Martinez—what had happened to her?

He had happened to her. The past two days in Granada had shown her a side to him she could never have imagined in a 'shallow playboy'. The day before, with its visit to the Alhambra, had demonstrated his deep knowledge and his love of history and culture. After the Nasrid palace they'd roamed the rest of the magnificent buildings and then visited the gardens, with their blossoming orange trees, seen the grandeur of the thousand-year-old cypress trees and gazed on the rose and myrtle bushes.

But it had been today that had constricted her lungs and

twisted her heartstrings. Because Rafael had insisted on accompanying her to the dog rescue centre, and once there he had shown a mixture of sensitivity, outrage, pragmatism and generosity that had astounded her. He'd listened to the plight of each animal and visited the kennels with her, approached every dog.

Cora's hand hovered over the gold dress and then she pulled it back. *Hang on.* Had she lost the plot and every single brain cell? Yes, Rafael had cared about the rescue dogs, but there was no correlation between that fact and her need to wear a dress with the wow factor. After all, any time she'd ever made an effort to impress before it had backfired horrendously and seared her soul.

There had been the disastrous boyfriend at university, who had courted and wooed her until she had finally succumbed and slept with him. After that he had refused all contact with her and she'd discovered that it had been done as part of an initiation dare—he had been given the challenge of adding a member of the aristocracy to the notches on his bedpost.

Then, of course, there had been Rupert. Most recently there had been the con artist posing as a journalist. There might not have been romance at stake, but she'd lost the Derwent diamonds as well as whatever small credibility she'd gained with her parents. So all in all a dismal record.

But Rafael was different.

'Tchaah.'

The snort dropped from her lips and shook her back to reality. That wasn't the point. The point was there was *no* point in wowing Rafael Martinez. The man had made it clear he did not wish to act on any attraction between them, and come to that neither did Cora. Rafael was dangerous—he had also made it abundantly clear relationships weren't his bag, and that even if they were, any

NINA MILNE   137

relationship with Rafael had the potential to destroy her. There would be a terrifying constant drive to live up to his extraordinarily high expectations accompanied by a wait for the inevitable time when he would move on to the next opportunity.

The thought made her shudder and prompted her to reach for the trusted grey dress.

Yet she felt a fizzle of disappointment as she entered the lounge, was aware of a foolish feeling of cowardice and an inability to meet his gaze. Instead she focused on the sleek leather lines of the furniture, on the cool sun-scented breeze that flew in through the open window from the dusky Granada night, along with the faint notes of a jazz trombone that lingered in the air and touched her with regret that she had chosen the path of safety.

'All ready.'

The falsetto brightness of her voice caused her to wince as she turned towards the door. She halted as a broad body blocked her path, her vision filled with the breadth of his chest, the triangle of tanned bare skin, the black silk of his shirt. Heaven help her, he smelled so good her head whirled.

Digging deep, she pulled up a smile, reminded herself that she was in *Granada*, for Pete's sake, about to see a flamenco show and eat gorgeous food. There really was nothing to regret or rue.

'Let's go! I'm really looking forward to dinner.'

'Good. I thought you'd enjoy it more than a swanky restaurant.'

'You thought right.'

As they walked through the bright tableau of Granada by night a warmth touched her at the fact that he had thought of her—she had little doubt that his usual dates would prefer an award-winning restaurant, a place to be seen and papped. That would be as important to them as the quality of the food.

'Here we are.'

Rafael came to a halt and Cora gazed at the unpretentious building. A small crowd of people was entering—a mix of all ages, some dressed up to the nines, others more casual, some old, some young. A pretty good representation of life.

As they entered the building they were led down a flight of twisting stairs lit by candles that flickered from cavities in the stone walls. Down, down, down into what looked as though it had originally been a cave. The domed stone ceiling curved above brightly laid tables packed together in rows in front of the stage. Once they were seated, drinks appeared as if by magic.

Cora sipped the red liquid and grinned. 'Sangria. Isn't that an abomination to vintners?'

He returned the smile as he raised his glass. 'It all depends on the wine. In fact I supply the wine here, so even though it's diluted with orange juice, filled with chopped oranges and limes and then chilled, that fact makes it more bearable.'

The words were a reminder that for all his playboy enjoyment of life he also ran a savvy business in an area that he loved.

'To Martinez wine.' She clinked her glass against his. 'And your next venture. I hope it works out.'

'So do I.'

'Why is it so important to you?' The words flew out before she could stop them, pulled out by the haunted look in his dark eyes.

For a moment she thought he might answer with the truth. Then music beat a tune from the stage and he leant back in his chair as if in relief.

'I told you, Cora. It's business.'

Frustration gripped her as she gazed at the neutrality of his features, the sudden remoteness in his stance.

Chill, Cora. It's nothing to do with you.

Yet she wanted to know—not out of idle curiosity but because she could sense his pain and she wanted to help. In the same way that every time she entered a dog rescue centre she sensed the hurt the animals had been through.

Get a grip. Was she really comparing Rafael to a rescue dog? Rafael Martinez did not need her help. Didn't need anything from her.

Time to focus on the stage.

It wasn't exactly a hardship. For the next hour the dancers and the music held her enthralled. The two female dancers, in their figure-hugging, flounced ankle-length dresses vibrant with polka dots, mesmerised her, their high heels clacking in time to the tempo and the words of the song as though they, the singer and the guitarist had some sort of inner connection. Cora's breath caught as the guitarist's fingers blurred, the lyrics of the song vibrated in the air and the dancers shimmied—the whole fusing into a crescendo of pure emotion.

To her own shock she realised that along with everyone else her feet were pounding the floor as she called out *'Ole!'* Every feeling was intensified. Her heart pulsed, and a giddy, heady sense of intense freedom filled her as the final notes lingered in the air. And then there was silence, a quietness of profound depth, almost spiritual, before applause broke out.

'That was…I can't come up with any words,' she said when the final cheer had died away and the performers had quit the stage. Around them the heightened atmosphere relaxed into an excited murmur of voices and the clink of glasses. 'I can't believe I got so carried away.' A chuckle fell from her lips. 'So un-English and so unladylike. My mother would be horrified.'

'Well, I'm not.' His voice whispered over her already sensitive skin and his dark eyes roamed over her face with appreciation and heat. 'I feel privileged to have seen you let go.'

Again.

The unspoken word was louder than if it had been yelled from the rooftops. A memory of how much she had let go during their kiss sent a cascade of heat through her whole body.

'I…I've had a great time. The whole day has been fantastic. I've had *fun*.' The idea almost novel.

'That's the idea.'

Suddenly the room felt overheated, and the temptation to reach out and touch him caused her to push her chair back. 'Please excuse me for a minute. Bathroom break. I'll be right back.'

Rafael watched as Cora made her way back to the table— she was so damned pretty that even the grey dress no longer had the power to mute her. Truth be told she looked a different person from the Cora who had been at the Derwent family dinner. The sun had given her face a touch of colour, her blue eyes held a sparkle and she walked with a confidence that her family seemed to suck from her. As for the way she had lost herself in the flamenco… It had shown him that Lady Cora Derwent had a fun-loving, decadent side to her that she seldom allowed to be on display.

It was a side she seemed to have walled off now. As she sat down he sensed her withdrawal as she picked up the menu and stared into the plastic pages as if it were the Holy Grail.

'What would you like?'

'I know it's a bit of a cliché, but I really want to try a proper authentic paella.'

'Sounds good to me.'

Once the food was ordered she cleared her throat, sipped her wine and then glanced across at him. 'I wanted to thank you for today…at the dog rescue centre.'

'You've already thanked me. And I've already told you there was no need. I'm happy if I've helped.'

The whole visit had been an eye-opener, in more ways than one. He'd admired Sally Anne Gregory, a petite Scottish dynamo who had a passion for animals in need that matched Cora's. And Cora had been transformed before his eyes as she went into action.

She had sat down, rolled up her sleeves and sorted out the admin backlog, had come up with innovative yet do-able strategies for raising awareness, updated social media accounts. Then they had visited the kennels. Anger and compassion threaded in his guts now as he thought about the dogs in care.

'This is just a drop in the ocean,' Cora had explained. 'But at least these dogs have hope.'

Cora had visited every dog, and to Rafael it had been a revelation. It was as though she had an uncanny link, an empathy, a lack of fear and a love for each of those dogs. Rafael had been truly shocked at the condition of some of the animals, and even more shocked to be presented with the statistics. He'd made some phone calls, transferred some money, and desperately tried to ignore the gaze of a dog called Dottie. An enormous Spanish Mastin-Shepherd cross, Dottie had been the only dog who'd seemed to zero in on him rather than Cora, her soulful brown eyes following his progress in mute appeal.

'I can't get Dottie out of my head,' he admitted now. 'I mean they were all worthy causes, but Dottie—for some reason she haunts me. She was so gentle, and to see her still being able to behold humans with kindness and affection after what she went through was humbling.'

'Dogs are intrinsically forgiving. That's why I like them

so much. And Dottie is on the right track—I think she can sense that to take revenge on all humans for what one person did would be wrong.'

'What about revenge on that one person? I would very much like the opportunity to spend some time alone with *him*.' When he thought about how Dottie had been hurt, neglected and abandoned his blood simmered.

Cora's turquoise eyes held sadness now. 'I don't understand how anyone can do what Dottie's owner did to her. And I wish there could be some sort of justice rather than vengeance. The two things are different. I think justice would be better served by showing him the truth of what he's done, making him understand and feel genuine remorse.'

'With people like that it's not possible. Sometimes vengeance is the only way to gain justice.'

'I don't want to believe that. Surely everyone is capable of change?' As she pulled her wine glass towards her she gave head a little shake, her red hair glinting in the twinkling lights of the restaurant. 'Anyway, maybe you should consider taking Dottie. She connected with you too. I could see it.'

An image came of the large sandy-coloured dog pawing at his leg as her brown eyes beseeched him before she sank down and rolled over for a tummy-rub. *For heaven's sake, Martinez.* That was all she wanted—any human touch, not his in particular.

'It wouldn't be fair on her. I don't have the sort of life-style that could accommodate a dog. I travel too much, I move around too much, I…' He was making too many excuses, and his defensiveness was on display in the rigidity of his body. 'I've never owned a dog before and I'm not about to start now.'

'Well, it's a shame—because you are definitely a dog person. Even Flash liked you. Remember?'

Flash. The dog Cora had been walking in the Cornish park at the outset of this fake marriage plan. It seemed a long time ago. Another time. Another place. The Cora who sat opposite him now was a far cry from the cold, aloof woman hunched on a park bench. The thought evoked a mix of emotion in his gut—the predominant one being an irrational wish that she had maintained that ice and distance.

Nuts. Just because Cora had turned out to be a warm person with hidden depths of character it made no odds to him.

Unbidden, his thoughts flew to his mother and her description of falling for Ramon, written in her bold, curved script in her final letter to Rafael.

When I first met him I didn't know who he was—couldn't have imagined his rank and wealth. When he told me I felt awed, but then I saw the person, the man beneath. And so love crept up on me, and made me believe that a happy-ever-after was possible. With a man who fascinated me, a man who made me laugh and made me care.

A man who had ultimately gone on to betray her—something she had once believed to be an impossibility.

'Rafael?'

A small frown creased Cora's forehead, and there was a question in her eye. He forced his expression to neutral, refocused on the conversation. 'I remember Flash. A Border Collie.'

'Flash doesn't like anyone much. You're a dog person.'

'That's as may be. But I can't commit to a dog. It wouldn't be fair to the dog.' So it was ludicrous for him to imagine Dottie huffing out a mournful sigh. For a start she couldn't hear him, and secondly she didn't understand

English because she was a *dog*, for Pete's sake. It was even more ridiculous to feel a sudden defensiveness at his apparent inability to commit to anything. There was nothing wrong with a desire to keep his life free and uncluttered, unfettered by ties.

'Why not?' Cora's tone was non-belligerent—eminently reasonable, in fact.

'Because a dog is an enormous commitment.'

'I get that, but if Dottie would bring you happiness and vice versa I think you could do it.' She leant forward, her features illuminated by the candlelight. 'I mean I know you live in both Spain and London, but you could bring Dottie to and fro. There are certain pet travel rules but they aren't that complicated. Dottie would have a passport, and she'd need to have up-to-date vaccinations. I wouldn't recommend travel by plane, but by ferry it should be OK. With your kind of money I'm sure you could do it in style. And for short trips you could afford to hire the best, most empathetic dog-sitter in the world. There are answers to everything—the point is that you could have Dottie if you really wanted to.'

As he listened to her for a fraction of a second the idea almost took hold. *Almost*. Before sanity prevailed. 'I prefer to keep my life uncomplicated and that sounds way too complicated for me. I like my life exactly as it is.'

'Then I won't say another word. You've already helped all those dogs so much with that bank transfer, to say nothing of the money you persuaded others to give. You should only give Dottie a home if it's what you really want, and if it's too big a commitment then so be it.'

Her sheer reasonableness brought him a strange wave of discomfort, alongside a funny sensation of loss, and it was a relief when the paella arrived—before he could let himself regret his own inability to give on a personal level as well as a monetary one.

'What about you?' he asked once the waiter had wished them *buen provecho* and moved away.

'What *about* me?'

'We've established that I can't have Dottie, but…'

'I can't either.' Sadness touched her face. 'I already have Prue and Poppy, and anyway right now it wouldn't be practical. I wish I could take them all in—or at least help find them all a home.'

'Why don't you? If you don't want to set up on your own you could go into partnership with Sally Anne.'

'Don't start that again.' A sweep of her hand at the heaped paella indicated her desire to change the subject. 'This looks delicious.'

Perhaps she was right—he should let it go. But he couldn't—not now he'd witnessed her in action. 'It does. And, yes, the food here is pretty authentic. The chef uses locally sourced ingredients. So it's not the best paella you can get in Spain but it's pretty high up there.'

He spooned a generous portion onto her plate and then onto his.

'So that closes the subject of food. As for the wine—it's from my vineyards, so I can vouch for an aromatic spicy taste that complements the flavour of the food. So that's that. *Why* won't you do what you want to do with your life?'

'I *am* doing what I want to do with my life.'

Rafael shook his head. 'I saw you with Sally Anne. I saw you with the dogs. I saw the way you tackled the administrative side of things *and* the ideas side. That's why I asked you to speak to people and ask for donations.'

'No, it wasn't. You thought they were more likely to donate if a lady asked them.'

'Partly. But I promise you—they may have listened because of your title, but they donated because of what you said. I'll lay you odds that they wouldn't have given a fraction of the amount to Kaitlin.'

Cora stilled, her fork in mid-air, en route to her lips. 'Don't be silly.'

'I'm not. They could hear your passion for this cause. You care about it. So, seriously, why not set up with Sally Anne? Or set up a rescue place of your own? Use the money you earn from this marriage. Make a difference.'

A look of wistfulness crossed her face, then she placed her fork down and shook her head. 'I can't.'

'Why not?'

'I have other obligations. To Derwent Manor. To my family. My parents wouldn't buy in to a dog rescue scheme. In fact they would be horrified. The one time I wanted to do a sponsored walk for a dogs' charity they were rendered almost speechless. They pointed out that any fundraising I did should benefit Derwent Manor.'

'And you agree with that? You won't put money *you've* earnt, fair and square through this marriage, into a dog rescue centre because your parents wouldn't approve?'

'It's not that. Actually, I need the money for something else.' Her gaze skittered from his, and her foot tapped the floor in patent discomfort.

Rafael frowned. When they had embarked on this deal he had known she needed money. He had assumed that, like any other woman of his acquaintance, she wanted it for clothes, jewellery, a luxury lifestyle. Now that idea seemed absurd. Yet maybe it wasn't—maybe he'd misread Cora completely and she *did* want the money to spend and enjoy and just didn't want to admit it. And who was he to judge that?

'It's your money—if you want to blow the lot on a yacht you can.'

Her eyes narrowed. 'I am not going to blow the money on anything. I need it to…'

She pressed her lips together, and he felt curiosity over-rule the idea that it was none of his business.

'To what?'

CHAPTER THIRTEEN

CORA STARED AT Rafael across the table and tried to apply the brakes to her vocal cords. It didn't matter what Rafael thought. Only it did.

Cora winced as discomfort tangled in her tummy. She loathed the idea that Rafael might even *think* she would rather spend the money on herself than use it for good. Especially when she remembered the size of the donation he'd made to Sally Anne.

'I need the money to pay a debt.'

As the words flew from her lips regret struck as surprise simultaneously raised his eyebrows.

'I didn't have you down as the type to get into debt.'

'I'm *not*. I've never been so much as overdrawn before—and, no, I don't have a chequered career as a serial gambler either.'

His frown deepened and she could almost see disbelief dawning in his eyes.

'It's OK, Cora. It's your money. You don't have to justify how you spend it to me.'

The problem was she would rather expose her stupidity than have him think she was like the shallow women he dated. Plus, perhaps she needed a jolt of reality—because for a few minutes she had almost believed it was possible to change her life's trajectory. So…

'A few months ago I was approached by a journalist. He

said he was called Tom Elkins and that he was new in the business and hoping to break into one of the magazines. He wanted to do a "Lady in the Limelight" piece about me, putting the unknown sister under the spotlight. It was a great fee, and I thought it would be a great opportunity to show my family that I could bring Derwent Manor some positive publicity. That I'd outgrown my tendency to mess up on important occasions.'

Pathetic—that was what it had been—her neediness, her patent delight in the attention, her selfishness in wanting to show everyone. Well, she'd got her comeuppance, all right.

'Long story short: he persuaded me to show him round the Manor, even the parts we don't open to the public, so he could get a proper overall feel of what being a Derwent means. Then he brought in Lucy Gerald, supposedly his photographer. A week later there was a break-in at the Manor and amongst other heirlooms the Derwent diamonds were stolen. Funnily enough I never heard from Tom again, and it turns out from his description and fingerprints that he is an expert thief.'

The memory of that discovery, the cold, hard stone of reality, the aching, stabbing guilt, the pain of her parents' shock, horror and disparagement, still made her blood run cold.

'Weren't they insured?'

'Not the diamonds. The insurance was too costly and Mum and Dad were confident that security was tight enough.'

'It's still foolish not to have insurance unless you are willing to accept the risk of loss.'

'It was my fault.'

Her parents had been in total agreement on that score, for sure.

'In hundreds of years no one has ever stolen anything from the Manor. Not so much as a teaspoon. Then I come along and with true Cora Derwent panache I pretty much unlock the safe for a pair of well-known thieves and con artists. Not surprisingly, my parents weren't very happy.'

Rafael didn't look that happy himself; his jaw was set hard. 'You made an innocent mistake—they took a calculated risk.'

'And I screwed up the odds with my stupidity.' Cora tilted her chin. 'I can't blame them for being disappointed. So when they made it clear they no longer wanted me to continue to work at Derwent Manor I knew what I had to do. Earn their trust back by repaying my debt.'

'But that would have taken you years.' Bafflement infused his tone.

'Yes. But so be it. I figured once I got together a good sum hopefully they would at least forgive me.'

'Then I came along with my proposal?'

'Yes. Now I can pay them back in full.' The words sent a wave of relief through her—the feeling of a weight being lifted. 'I know that is the right thing to do.'

Rafael pushed his empty plate away from him and picked up his wine, cradled the glass in his large hands. 'I can see that. I don't understand why your parents were so harsh, but I can see why you feel the need to give them the money. But then what?'

Cora frowned. 'What do you mean?'

'After that. When you have repaid the debt, what will you do then?'

'Hopefully they will give me my job back and life can return to normal.' The plan that had filled her with such hope just days before seemed suddenly a little flat, and annoyance skittered through her. Somehow Rafael had messed with her head.

To her relief the waiter materialised and engaged in conversation in rapid Spanish with Rafael as he cleared the plates. Thank goodness—now they would leave the res-

taurant and this conversation behind, and it was undoubt-
edly time to resume the 'smiles and platitudes' strategy.

'Please, can you tell the waiter that the food was delicious and I have had a lovely evening?'

'Actually, the evening isn't over. Juan has explained
that the chef would like us to have dessert on the house.
A speciality, Lagrimas de Boabdil—the tears of Boabdil.'

Just flipping great.

Rafael studied Cora's expression as she dug her spoon into
the honey and raspberry dessert. It seemed clear that she
would like to terminate the conversation and instinct told
him she was right. Her life choices were *zip* to do with
him. But curiosity alongside frustration begged a question.

'Why do you want everything to revert to normal? Why
not stay here and work with Sally Anne? Or get a job with
an animal charity? Surely your parents would prefer you
to do something that makes you happy rather than spend
your life in a role that doesn't fulfil you.'

But even as he said the words he knew it didn't work
like that—this was a family who had sabotaged their
daughter's wedding day...had let her marry a man they
believed would discard her...

'The Derwent family don't rock and roll like that. It's
a family business. You are born into it and you work for
it. That's how it is and I can't buck the trend.'

'Why not? You can't spend your life doing something
you don't want to do.' Especially for a family Rafael was
beginning to believe were on a par with the de Guzmans.

Leaning forward he tried to convey the importance of
his words. 'You said it yourself yesterday. You believe in
the right of the individual. You don't *have* to do what every
Derwent has done since time immemorial. You can stand
up for what you want. Your parents would come round.'

Her lips parted and he thought she would perhaps

vouchsafe the truth—a real explanation. Instead she smiled a smile that seemed expressly designed to humour him.

'Maybe you're right. Maybe one day.'

'No.' His fork dropped to his plate with a clatter as he exhaled a sigh heavy with frustration. 'Because one day may never come.'

How could he make her understand that she mustn't give up on her own life? He didn't want this new Cora, vibrant and passionate, to morph back to that cool, aloof, muted Cora, burdened by familial obligation.

'I *know* this. My mother was diagnosed with advanced cancer before she was forty—her chance to live her life was snatched from her.'

It felt strange to say the words—words he hadn't uttered for so very long, words that brought his mother's face into focus, reminding him of the gut-wrenching sheer panic and misery and the fear that had assailed him when she'd broken the news.

Cora reached across the table and covered his hand with both of hers. The warmth of her touch gave him a comfort he shouldn't want, and yet it consoled him.

'I'm sorry. *So* sorry. How old were you?'

'Fourteen.'

'So that memory you have—that happy memory of you and her at the fairground…?'

'Is from the final months of her life—she knew it would be the last birthday she'd spend with me. But she made sure it was a memorable one. We had a wonderful day—and it's how I like to remember her.' Blonde hair flying in the breeze, her face creased with laughter—having fun, full of life.

Cora blinked and he could see a tear quiver on the end of her lashes.

'So what happened to you?' she asked. 'Did you have family to take you in?'

'I had family, but they didn't want to take me in and I
didn't want to go to them. They didn't like my mother—
thought she was above herself. So the upshot was that I
went into care.'

'Oh!'

'Don't look so aghast. It was for the best. I was already
on the slippery slope to screwing up my life. I'd been bunk-
ing off school, had got involved in petty crime to make
money, so that I could make Mum's last months at least a
bit luxurious.' He shook his head as regret bit at him. 'A
box of chocolates, a bottle of cheap perfume... Nothing
compared to what I could have given her if she'd lived. But
she was so appreciative of each and every gift.'

Cora's fingers squeezed his hand.

'I wanted to make good. I'd promised her I would get
my life back on track and live it to the full. That was made
easier by my carers. They were good people—experienced
foster carers. I went back to school, I caught up, and I got
into technology. And then I invented that gizmo that made
me millions.'

'Your mum would have been so proud of you. And I believe—I really do—that somehow she knows that you did
good. And not because you made bucketloads of money.
Because you kept your promise to her to get your life on
track and live your life to the full. Thank you for telling
me, Rafael.'

'I told you because I want you to see the importance of
seizing the day. You need to make your dreams happen
now. Promise you'll think about it.'

'I promise.'

Rafael exhaled a breath and realised that Cora's hands
were still wrapped around his. Realised that he had shared
way more than he had intended, and that this dinner had
veered into a dangerous area. He should have terminated
this conversation long ago. No more. Time to remind Cora

and himself that this was a business marriage and a business honeymoon.

'Good.' Pulling his hand gently away, he turned to look for the waiter. 'It may be an idea to think quickly. My plan is to put out a feeler to Don Carlos tomorrow and see if he is now willing to negotiate.'

An expression flitted across her face—a disappointment that she masked so fast he couldn't be sure it had even existed.

'Won't he think it's strange that you're thinking about business on your honeymoon?' Her eyes focused on her plate as she pushed the last crumbs into a small heap with her fork.

'No. He'll understand that, honeymoon or not, I won't want to lose out on the vineyard.'

Relief surged over him that he'd got his plan back on track. Yet that relief was lined with a sense of impending loss, a shadow of the way he had felt when he had realised he would lose his mother. A danger warning sounded and was heeded—never again would he open himself up to that level of pain.

CHAPTER FOURTEEN

CORA SHIFTED ON the sofa, stretched her legs down over the leather surface, stared at the pages of her book and wished that she could focus on the characters. But she couldn't—she had tried and failed for the past two days to lose herself amongst the pages.

Two days during which she'd barely seen Rafael. Ever since their dinner in the flamenco restaurant he had withdrawn, spent most of his time engrossed in work—presumably on the vineyard deal. There had been no more sightseeing—he had pointed out that real honeymooners would enjoy staying in. But the words had been uttered dispassionately, with no hint of the attraction or the closeness that had characterised their first two days. And she, fool that she was, missed both the attraction and the closeness.

The thought filled her with an urge to hurl the book across the room in sheer irritation.

Just then the door opened and Rafael entered. *Breathe.* Cora concentrated on her novel, refused to look up. Until ignorance was impossible to simulate anymore because he stood right next to her, the muscular length of denim-clad leg tantalising her gaze.

'Sorry to interrupt. I just wanted to let you know I've heard from Don Carlos's man of business—I've set up a meeting with Don Carlos tomorrow in Madrid to sign the paperwork for the vineyard.'

Despite the fact that she had expected some progress the words hit her with shocking impact, and she swung her legs over the leather seat. *Too soon.* The thought reverberated through her brain. *Too soon.*

Somehow she pulled a smile to her face. 'That's fantastic!' Because it was—*of course it was.* She surveyed his set expression—she could see no sign of triumph or even a smidgeon of happiness. 'Isn't it...?'

'Yes. But I won't fully believe it until the title deeds are in my hands.' He scrubbed a hand down his face. 'Anyway, whatever happens with the vineyard tomorrow, this marriage charade can end. I'll transfer the balance of your fee and you can pay your parents back.'

The idea should have her cartwheeling around the room, but still the words *too soon* tolled in her head. *Madness.*

'That's wonderful.' Squashing down the urge to leave it at that, she dug down and located a modicum of courage. 'And it seems like a good time to tell you that I *did* keep my promise and I *have* thought deeply about my future and the idea of a dog rescue centre. I've decided against it.'

His dark eyes bored into her as if they could read her inner soul and he sat down opposite her. 'Can I ask why?'

Damn. She'd hoped that he would just accept her decision, but she'd known that if he asked she owed him the truth. Rafael deserved that—he cared about her future because of the demons of his own past, and she wanted him to know why she couldn't change her life.

'Because I need to follow my ultimate dream. I need to prove to my parents, to myself, that I am a proper Derwent. All my life that's what I've striven for and I've never achieved it.'

'I don't get it. You seem like model daughter material.'

'If only! I've never managed that...' His dark gaze was focused solely on her, and somehow the words came easily. 'Not even as a baby. Mum didn't find out she was expecting twins until late on in the pregnancy and the whole idea freaked her out. Maybe if she'd delivered two Kaitlins or if I'd been a boy it would have been OK. But I was another girl, and I was a sickly, ugly scrap—whereas Kaitlin was bonny and beautiful. Kaitlin fed easily and never cried. To my parents it must have seemed that Kaitlin had got all the good and I'd got all the bad.'

How many times had she pictured the revulsion on her parents' face? Sometimes she wondered if it were a latent memory.

'They couldn't bond with me. I've always known that and I don't blame them. The Derwents set a lot of store in perfection, you see—looks, intelligence…it's all part of our breeding. I'm the ugly duckling who remained an ugly duckling.'

'No.' He shook his head. 'You were not an ugly duckling. You were a baby. And as a baby, as a child, as their daughter, you deserved your parents' love.'

'I think they used all their love up on Kaitlin and Gabriel—they were golden children and I was an unwanted spare. But they did at least do their duty by me.'

'That isn't enough.'

'Maybe. But that isn't the point. The point is I can't just go off and set up a dog rescue charity, or a dog-walking company. All that would do is prove to them that they were right about me all along. I *will* show them that I am a true Derwent, I *will* win their approval, and I *will* change their minds. And the best way for me to do that is to work for the Derwent estate.

'Stop!' The word sounded as if it were torn from his throat. 'Don't, Cora. Don't waste your life trying to change them. People don't change.'

'You don't know that.'

'Yes, I do. My mother spent a decade in limbo, grieving for the love of her life—my father—a man who abandoned and betrayed her. Always hoping he'd come back, hoping he'd change. Well, he didn't—and she wasted her life hoping for something that was never going to happen.'

Cora could almost taste his frustration and doubt touched her. The image of his mother, waiting for a love that never materialised, chilled her with sadness. But...

'I can't let myself believe that.' How could she when this was what she had striven for all her life? 'Maybe there are facts that you don't know, Rafael. About your father. Maybe your mother was right to wait for him. Maybe...'

'Maybe he was a weak, cowardly bastard.'

'You don't know that.'

'Yes, I do.'

He rose to his feet, as if the very idea of his father forced some sort of movement, and paced the carpet to stand by the marble mantelpiece.

'My mother left a letter with a solicitor to be given to me when I was thirty. In it she revealed my father's identity. I traced him and I found out that he left us to marry someone else. But he didn't have the guts to tell her face to face—he left that job to someone else. Sent that someone to make sure my mother didn't cause trouble. He turned up with a bunch of goons and terrorised her. Hurt her. Vandalised all her belongings and threw us onto the street with nothing. I was five, and all I can remember is the feeling of sheer helplessness, my inability to defend her.'

Horror stole Cora's breath. 'That...that's awful.'

'Yes. Yet my mother persisted in her belief in him and wasted so many years.' He took in a deep breath. 'Don't let that happen to you with your parents. Don't see good where there is none to see.'

Right now all she could see was a vision of the five-year-old Rafael, forced to watch as his mother was beaten and hurt, and it tore at her heartstrings. Without thought she stood and moved towards him. Closed the gap and put her arms around him, her hands against the strength of his back. His body remained rigid, so she put her cheek against his chest, felt the pounding of his heart, heard his exhalation before he allowed his body to relax.

'I'm sorry for what you and your mum went through. It sucks. Big-time.'

It could have been seconds they stood there, it could have been minutes, but slowly an awareness of how close they were, of the breadth of his chest, the accelerated beat of his heart, the woodsy scent of him, pervaded her being. It filled her with a longing so intense it almost hurt. Not almost. It *did* hurt, and the knowledge gave her the strength to move backwards.

But now she could see him—see the awareness that mirrored hers, the heat in his dark eyes as he looked at her. And the whisper of an idea slipped into her brain, urged her to live in the here and now and take the opportunity to grasp what she wanted.

Madness. Say something, anything, before you do something stupid.

'How about I make us a farewell dinner tonight? I'll sort it out. I can pop out and get some food, no problem, and then...' *Put some distance between us.*

But distance wasn't what she wanted. If only she could read his mind. Did he regret what he'd shared? Or was he too caught in this web of misplaced awareness and the knowledge that after tomorrow they would most likely never see each other again.

The idea banded her chest in sudden panic.

'OK. That sounds great,' he said after an almost imperceptible pause.

'Great. I'll head to the shops, then.'

Did she dare? The question swirled and tapped and danced around her as she left the apartment and stepped onto sun-dappled pavement, inhaling the now familiar scents of Granada. Orange blossom, mingled with the mouthwatering scent of fried *churros* that triggered the remembered tang of melted chocolate and pastry on her tongue.

Did she dare? As she purchased a selection of pâté, cheese, olives and bread the idea of seduction cast its magical spell. *Could she do it?* The knowledge that this was her last chance urged her to throw caution to the wind, to risk certain heartbreak and seize this opportunity. Would she be strong enough to play by his rules? Strong enough to say goodbye with dignity and no regrets? After all, she knew Rafael wasn't for her—he was as far from Joe Average as it was possible to be. And she knew she wasn't for him.

There was no way in hell, heaven or earth that a woman like herself could keep Rafael for more than a brief interlude. A woman like her could never be more than an opportunity to him—but maybe in the here and now that was enough.

So this time as she got ready for dinner there was no hesitation as she pulled the shimmering gold dress from the wardrobe and laid it on the bed. She washed her hair and left it loose.

Half an hour later she gazed at her reflection—it was hard not to see an imaginary Kaitlin standing next to her, in the same dress, looking more...

Not this time.

Cora scrunched her eyes shut, reopened them and glared at her reflection, remembering Rafael's words.

'You aren't a pale imitation of Kaitlin and you don't have to live in her shadow. It's your life. Live it. Keep the dress for another occasion, another time when you do feel comfortable in it. Because you will wow the world or the man you wear it for.'

So 'comfortable' might be pushing it, and she didn't

care about the world, but the desire to wow Rafael was bone-deep.

Before she could change her mind she headed through to the dining area. Desperate shyness twisted in her tummy, along with the ice-cold realisation that Rafael might not even remember the dress.

He was immersed in a document, scanning it with ferocious concentration.

'Hey.' Her voice was too high-pitched as she stood there.

He looked up—and his double-take, the way he scrambled to his feet, his jaw ever so slightly dropped as he gazed at her, filled her with a fizz of anticipation.

'You look even better in that dress than I imagined you would.'

His voice was slow and appreciative, reminiscent of expensive chocolate and malt whisky, and she knew the dress spoke for itself.

'And I was right about the wow factor. You look spectacular.'

Pure feminine triumph streamed through her veins, filling her with heady power.

'Thank you. I'll bring the food through in a minute, but I wanted to talk first.'

'OK.' A few strides brought him towards her. 'Shoot.'

'I...'

As she looked up at him, absorbed the aquiline features, the jut of his jaw, the clear dark gaze that blazed with desire, saw the tiny, barely noticeable scar by his left eyebrow, the breath-stealing glory of him, her carefully rehearsed speech faded away.

Stepping forward, she rested her palms on his chest, stood on tiptoe, slid her hands up onto his shoulders and pressed her lips against his. She revelled in the sensation, in the tang of coffee, the sheer buzz that rocketed through her pulse.

His hands encircled her waist as he deepened the kiss and she gave herself up to the vortex of pleasure, soaring free from all her worries and fears and existing purely in the moment.

She only came down to earth when she realised he'd ended the kiss, though he still held her body close to his.

'Cora, are you sure…?' he began, his breathing ragged, his deep voice strained.

'More sure than I've ever been.' She held his gaze, even though her legs threatened weakness at the heat in his eyes—a heat that promised untold pleasures to come. 'I had a whole speech prepared, but what it comes down to is that I want to seize this moment, this opportunity. This is *it*, Rafael. After tomorrow we will go our separate ways—and I would always regret not doing this. If that's what you want too?'

'Yes. It is what I want too.'

His deep voice sent a shiver down her spine all the way to the tips of her toes, and then she gave a sudden squeak as in one deft movement he scooped her up into his arms.

CHAPTER FIFTEEN

RAFAEL OPENED HIS eyes and stared up at the pristine white ceiling of his bedroom. In that instant of waking, he felt drowsy contentment wrap around him like a blanket. Cora's head rested on his chest, and the silky smoothness of her hair tempted his fingers. He gently entwined them in the sun-kissed red strands.

She opened her eyes and he smiled. 'Morning.'

'Morning,' she murmured, and for a sleepy heartbeat she snuggled into him with a languorous smile.

Then reality smote him. Morning brought with it his meeting with Don Carlos. The night was over—and there would be no more like it.

His thoughts were mirrored in her expression, in the sudden withdrawal in her eyes, in her abrupt movement to sit up, the sheet clutched to her chest.

'Right,' she said. 'You need to get to the airport. I'll get coffee on the go.'

For an insane moment near reluctance kept him still. What was *wrong* with him? This was what he had worked toward for over two and a half decades. The idea of revenge had fuelled him, and now it was so nearly in his grasp.

'That sounds good. Thank you.'

Half an hour later Cora handed him a coffee and looked him over. 'You look great,' she said. 'Good luck.'

A moment's hesitation and she stood on tiptoe and

kissed his cheek. The so familiar scent of her made him close his eyes for a heartbeat, in a sudden unlooked-for ache. *Enough*. Right now he needed to be focused. Don Carlos was not to be trusted and he needed to be in complete command of the situation.

He should be savouring this moment. Yet throughout the plane journey images of Cora pervaded his mind. The soft gurgle of her laugh. The passion they'd shared. Skin against skin. The texture of her lips. The silken smoothness of her red hair.

As the private jet began its descent Rafael pulled his thoughts to order. *Enough*. Cora didn't belong here, no longer had a place in his life. Steel determination banded his chest—today he would finally get the revenge he'd sworn to achieve all those years ago.

The chauffeured car negotiated Madrid's traffic-laden streets, headed towards the city's business district, epitomised by the soaring four-tower skyscrapers that dominated the skyline.

Once there he alighted and a cold burning filled him—a sudden desire to forget this civilised vengeance and simply storm the Duque de Aiza's bastion, grab Don Carlos by the throat. *No*. That would not gain him what he wanted—he wanted to see the humiliation on Don Carlos's face when he realised he'd been duped, that he'd handed his land over to the 'illegitimate, tainted son of a whore' he'd terrorised twenty-five years before.

It was almost a surprise to see how calm his features were in the chrome-edged mirror of the elevator that carried him to Don Carlos's lair. And then there he was again, in the inner sanctum where he'd been months ago.

'Rafael. We meet again.' The elderly Spaniard remained seated in his ornate wooden chair behind a dark mahogany desk.

'We do. I understand that you have reconsidered my proposal for the vineyard?'

'I have.' The Duque pushed a document across the desk. 'I think you'll find all is in order.'

Rafael stepped forward and picked up the papers.

'I suppose I will be the first of many who will negotiate with you now you have married into a title. You did well to choose Cora Derwent—I doubt anyone else would have had you. Kaitlin wouldn't have given you the time of day.'

'I'm sorry. I'm not sure I understand.'

Chill, Rafael. No doubt he wants to goad you.

'Come, come. You are using her—I know that and so do you. Does she believe you love her? Or does she *know* that all you want is acceptance into the upper echelons of society? I'm not criticising you—I applaud your acumen. You picked the less attractive, mousy one—the one who wouldn't say boo to the proverbial goose. Excellent choice. You can manipulate Cora and no doubt school her into accepting your infidelities, accepting being used with good grace. Her family have used her for years. So, as I said, you did well to choose such malleable material. It has certainly won you this vineyard. I can at least know that one day my land will go to a child with Derwent blood in its veins.'

Bile rose in his throat. Don Carlos, Duque de Aiza, the grandfather he loathed, was *applauding* him for his use of Cora, and the idea of his grandfather's approval turned his stomach. The way he spoke of Cora, of the woman he loved, made anger pulse in his veins.

Loved.

Rafael reached out a hand to steady himself against the dark wood of the desk.

Loved.

The idea impacted on him in all its inevitability—the knowledge was absolute and true. He *loved* his wife, and to use her was an impossibility.

So many thoughts freewheeled in his brain…a plethora of emotions twisted his guts. It was imperative that he got out of this godforsaken office, away from this bitter, envenomed man.

'I've changed my mind.'

'Excuse me?'

'I've changed my mind.'

Rafael barely recognised the croak of his own voice. The shocked disbelief on Don Carlos's face should have caused him satisfaction, but his brain was too busy imploding.

'I no longer wish to buy your vineyard.'

With that Rafael swivelled and left the office, barely registering the *swoosh* of the lift doors or its descent, or his arrival on the pavements of the city.

'I'll walk,' he told his driver.

Perhaps the air would clear his head and show him that this epiphany had been no more than illusion. How had it happened? How had Cora wriggled right under every single one of his defences? Though perhaps a better question would be how could he undo the damage—push her out so he could re-barricade his heart?

Panic set his head awhirl and he increased his stride. Love was not for him—he would *not* give Cora that power over him. So somehow he had to purge himself of this unwanted emotion. Yet there was a part of him that wanted to shout it from the rooftops—run straight to Cora and tell her. *Fool.* Was this how his mother had felt about Ramon Aiza—this heady, out of control, terrifying sensation? Even maybe the way Ramon had once felt for Emma? This so-called love that led to tragedy.

Well, he would withstand it—as his parents must have wished *they* had had the strength to do. His feet pounded the pavement. Love made you weak, and he would not succumb to its pervasive power.

* * *

Cora paced—she now knew that the lounge of Rafael's Madrid apartment was fifteen paces by seventeen. Also that it *was* possible to eat her own weight in chocolate.

Where was Rafael? Surely his meeting with Don Carlos couldn't have taken this long?

Her nails dug into her palms. What if he hadn't got the vineyard—what if it was some sort of underhand ploy by the Duque? In which case she could almost taste Rafael's rage and—worse—his humiliation. Cora didn't know why this vineyard mattered so much, but she suspected it was wrapped up in a desire to prove something to Don Carlos. So if that man had hurt Rafael in any way, Cora would... She wasn't sure what she'd do, but it would involve marching down to his office to give him a piece of her mind.

The idea stopped her in her tracks—she, timid, gauche Cora Derwent, was able to envisage bearding Don Carlos in his lair in defence of Rafael. Maybe she should have offered to attend the meeting—to emphasise their togetherness.

The sadness that she had tried so hard to ignore all day descended in an unstoppable wave. Sadness that last night had been the grand finale of their marriage contract. That there could be no more togetherness. But the night had given her memories, an experience that she would treasure for ever.

The click of his key in the door caused her to spin as the noise of his feet on the marble floor of the hall told of his arrival.

There was a pause, and then the door opened and Rafael stood in the arch. For a second she was sure something was wrong. There was a set to his features, a slight pallor under the Mediterranean hue. Then his lips turned up into a smile.

'How did it go?'

'Don Carlos agreed to sell the vineyard to me.' There was a curious flatness to his voice, though his smile widened.

'That is fantastic. You must be thrilled.' Yet she could feel her forehead scrunching into a frown of disquiet.

As if sensing it, he shrugged. 'I am—but an hour in that man's company makes me want to boil myself in disinfectant.'

'You need never see him again. The main thing is that you've got what you wanted. Don't let Don Carlos spoil it—not after all the effort you put in.'

'You're right.' He pushed himself off the doorjamb in one lithe movement and headed towards his laptop. 'And the same goes for you. I'll transfer the final balance now and then you're free. Free to return home.' His dark head was angled so he could see the screen, his expression hidden. 'Free to discharge your debt and win back your job.'

She watched as his dextrous fingers flew over the keyboard and panic assailed her. Because those words that should have been magical had left her cold. Instead of anticipation at her return to the Derwent fold she felt emptiness, a precipitate sense of loss. Because she didn't want to leave Rafael.

No. Please, no.

There was no way she could have fallen for Rafael Martinez—that was unacceptable.

Rafael did not want her love. He'd wanted her title, and now that commodity was used up he would be ready to move on to the next opportunity. It was the way he lived his life—free and uncluttered—and she had nothing to offer against that. She could never be enough for him, just as she had never been enough for her parents. She would *not* love him—would not allow herself to.

'Cora?'

And yet as she turned to face him the words strained to

be released, telling her to throw dignity to the wind and tell him the truth. But sudden fear paralysed her vocal cords. How could she bear rejection from him?

Rafael Martinez was out of her league—on a different playing field altogether. He was a man whose father had abandoned him in the cruellest way possible, whose mother had died after the waste of a decade mourning her lost love. Little wonder the idea of love was anathema to him. Maybe one day he'd meet a woman capable of making him change his mind, but she wasn't that woman. Rafael needed someone who could match his extraordinary energy, his love of life—someone who could leash his power. A beautiful, attractive, strong woman. Not her.

They had a deal and she would not renege on it. Any more than on the deal she had made with herself. To play by his rules and leave with her pride intact. With her memories of her time with him unsullied.

His expression was shuttered, though for an instant she thought concern lit the darkness of his eyes. *Pull it together.* If there was ever a time to resurrect cool, aloof Cora it was now.

'Sorry. I was miles away. I'm all packed—I just need to sort a flight.'

'Whenever you're ready. The money is in your account.'

There was nothing in his tone to indicate that he felt any regret, even a hint of sadness at this ending. If anything she had the impression he couldn't wait to be shot of her. And why not? *Get with it.* This was how Rafael Martinez rocked and rolled—he was a playboy, after all, and he'd never once tried to make her believe otherwise.

'Thank you. I'm glad this deal has worked out for us both.'

He rose from the desk and her breath caught in her throat—if he so much as touched her hand she would unravel, and right now it was imperative that she left before her pride cracked along with her heart.

Stepping backwards, she managed, 'Before I go we'd better get the story straight on our break-up.'

'I'll issue a statement—something along the lines of, "It is with sadness that Lady Cora Derwent and Rafael Martinez announce that their marriage is unsustainable. Once the romantic whirlwind wore off the couple realised that in fact they have very little in common and have decided to call it a day. The split is entirely amicable and they wish each other well."'

Unsustainable. Very little in common. Each word was like an individual bullet to her heart.

'Perfect. So now that's sorted I'll be on my way.'

No matter if she had to camp overnight, waiting for a flight, it would be better than remaining here. Digging deep, she pulled a smile to her lips, forced back tears of pain and humiliation.

'Thanks for everything. I hope life brings you many more opportunities.'

A strange self-mocking smile twisted his lips, but then he stepped forward and his expression morphed, and for a heartbeat he looked like *her* Rafael.

'Thank you. And *I* hope your parents start to appreciate and love you the way you deserve to be loved.'

His arms closed around her in a final hug so bittersweet her very soul ached.

CHAPTER SIXTEEN

IT WAS AN ache that persisted throughout her journey back to England, where the plane descended through grey, gloomy, rain-laden skies. A miserable train journey later and Cora braced herself as she approached Derwent Manor, gazing at the imposing pile of bricks and stone, the landscaped curve of the gardens, and trying and failing to feel even a flicker of pride or happiness at her heritage.

There was little point in putting off the inevitable, and despite her yearning to go and find Poppy and Prue she made her way to the library to find her parents.

The Duchess looked up from the table, where she sat surrounded by piles of photograph albums.

'Cora. What are *you* doing here?' Irritation sparked in her emerald eyes. 'We're having a dinner for Prince Frederick and Kaitlin and a few others. In fact I was just looking for some photos of Kaitlin as a child to show Frederick. It really is not a good time for you to be here—I don't want this dinner to go wrong, and I certainly don't need the Prince to remember our connection with Rafael Martinez.'

'You don't need to worry about that.' Cora blinked back tears. 'The marriage is officially over.'

Her parents exchanged glances and then the Duke gave a crack of laughter. 'Well, that's a record—even for you, Cora.'

'But no matter,' his wife said. 'The prenup still stands, and that's what matters.'

'Really?' Cora stared at them, realising that they weren't going to ask her how she was—didn't care about the abject misery her expression held.

'Really.' Her father rolled his eyes. 'The man is an oik—low-born, base scum who grew up in squalor. You've besmirched our name with that marriage, but that will be compensated for if it benefits the family coffers. Given the amount your stupidity with that journalist cost, I assume you're planning to hand over the cash?'

Expectant silence filled the air, and for a heartbeat the habit of Cora's lifetime nearly kicked in. *This* was why she had married Rafael—for this moment, the moment when she handed over the money, paid off her debt. Approval would dawn in her mother's emerald-green eyes, and a genuine smile would curl her father's lips. A true Derwent wouldn't hesitate—would hand over Rafael's money and feel good.

Yuck! There was no way she could do it. Her nails clenched into her palms as she looked at her parents and felt as if she was truly seeing them for the first time. Perhaps this was what love did to you—true love.

An icy rage possessed her, gave her courage. 'No. I'm not planning on handing over the cash. Rafael Martinez is worth a hundred Derwents and I'd be proud to stay married to him. I love him. Love doesn't depend on someone's birth or blood, or what they look like, or how socially acceptable they are. It depends on their inner worth. In which case, forget a hundred—Rafael is worth a *thousand* Derwents. Either way, I don't see why he should line the Derwent coffers. So I plan to give his money back. As for my stupidity—I fully acknowledge that and I will pay you back what I can, *when* I can. That I promise.'

The Duchess rose to her feet and Cora forced herself

to remain still, not to back off at the look of incandescent rage on her mother's face.

'I always knew you weren't a true Derwent. From the moment of your birth I knew you must be some throw-back, some—'

'Stop!'

Cora spun round, realised she hadn't even heard the library door open to admit Kaitlin.

'Enough.'

Her sister stepped forward to stand by her side, her skin leeched of colour.

'Cora is my twin—she is as true a Derwent as I am. So please stop this *now*. Cora is your daughter and—'

The Duke shook his head. 'And *as* our daughter she needs to behave the way our daughter should.'

Cora turned to her sister and smiled, truly touched that for the first time ever Kaitlin had jumped off the fence and offered support. 'It's OK, Kait.' Stepping away from her sister, she approached her parents. 'I'm sorry that you feel my actions are wrong, but I am behaving in the way that feels right to *me*. In a way that makes me feel good about myself. I'll be in touch.'

With that she turned and headed for the library door, aware that Kaitlin was close behind her.

'Where will you go?' her sister asked, once they had exited the Manor.

'I'm not sure yet. Somewhere I can take Poppy or Prue.'

A welcome numbness seemed to have settled over her, blanketing her from consideration of her actions. The spur that had driven her for so long no longer drove her and she felt only emptiness, an abyss made worse by the pain of wanting Rafael. The instinctive temptation to go to him for sanctuary nigh on overwhelmed her even as she recognised the sheer stupidity of that thought.

Rafael Martinez did not want her.

Kaitlin's beautiful face creased into a frown of concern. 'Take my car. Do you need money or...?'

'I'll be fine, Kait. I promise. Now, you'd better go and get ready for Prince Frederick and that dinner. There's no point making Mum and Dad even angrier.'

There was a pause, and then Kaitlin pulled her into an awkward hug before she headed back to the Manor.

Two months later

Cora approached Ethan and Ruby Caversham's London house. *Right.* The same rules applied as had applied for the past eight weeks. No matter what, she would *not* ask about Rafael. This lunch was supposed to be a pleasant social event with two people who had proved to be true friends. Friends who had given her sanctuary in Cornwall until press interest in her marriage break-up had died down and then given her a job at the Caversham Foundation in London.

Best of all, they had asked no questions. Or at least they hadn't until now. But there had been a certain something in Ruby's tone when she'd issued the lunch invitation that had made Cora suspect a hidden agenda. So here she was, hovering outside whilst considering retreat.

The front door opened and Ruby came out. 'Cora. I am *so* glad you're here. Ethan, you can stand down...' she called over her shoulder. 'Operation Kidnap Cora is no longer necessary.'

A genuine smile tipped her lips, though envy panged as Ethan came out and looped an easy arm round his wife's waist.

'Welcome, Cora. And many thanks for all you're doing at the office.'

'You're very welcome.'

'No more talk about work, Ethan Caversham!' Ruby

ordered in a severe tone totally alleviated by the look of adoration she cast on her husband. 'Come on in, Cora.'

Cora followed the Cavershams down the spacious book-lined hall and into a lounge that oozed an air of comfort and cosiness, with its overstuffed sofas, soft cushions, bean bags and bright paintings.

'This is gorgeous.'

'Thank you.' Ruby's sapphire eyes sparkled. 'Ethan and I want it to feel like a home. Its early days yet, but hope-fully, if one day we get accepted as adopters, I want to have the homiest home imaginable. And in the meantime some of those teens we're helping come round sometimes—it's really lovely. I mean, they pretend it's no big deal but it is. A lot of them live in residential homes and we want them to have somewhere else to go. In fact we're going to con-vert the basement into a teen den.'

Cora felt warmth and admiration touch her—Ruby *cared*, and so did Ethan. They worked together to bring good into others' lives, worked at something they both be-lieved in and felt passionate about.

'But enough of us,' Ruby said. 'What I really want to know is how *you* are? Not workwise, but how *you* are.'

'Fine…'

If you didn't count the number of minutes in the day she wasted on Rafael Martinez, remembering the way his genuine smile lit his eyes, his tendency to scrub his hand down his face when he was annoyed, his scent, his…

Ruby's dark blue eyes met hers. 'Really?'

'Of course.'

After all, once she got over Rafael she *would* be fine—she'd probably also be grey-haired and in her dotage, but hey-ho.

'I've got started on my plans for setting up a dog rescue centre too. Thank you both so much for that brainstorm-ing session—it really helped.'

Cora felt a fizz of excitement at the thought of her project. She'd thought it all through. Her determination to pay her parents back hadn't diminished, but if she could set up the charity in such a way as to earn a salary from it, and supplement that with dog-walking and maybe some part-time work for the Cavershams, she truly believed she could do it.

'Any time,' Ethan said as he paced the room.

Ruby glanced at her watch with a small frown and cast a glance at Ethan that clearly constituted some sort of telepathic conversation. 'Ethan, could you check the lunch? It should be nearly ready. Cora and I will just chill in here.'

Ethan hesitated, rubbing the back of his neck as he eyed his wife. 'Rube…'

There was a warning note to his voice that caused his wife to shake her head at him.

'It's OK, Ethan. I know what I'm doing.'

Cora frowned, watching as Ethan exited the room. 'Ruby, what is going on? Is there a problem? Ethan only paces when he's uncomfortable about something.'

The dark-haired woman sat back and exhaled, blowing her fringe off her forehead. 'There isn't a problem as such. Or at least I *hope* it's not a problem.'

'What is it?'

'Rafael will be here soon. He's asked us to arrange this because he doesn't want to risk any press attention. Or at least that's what he said. I think he was worried that if he asked you directly you'd refuse. That's why he didn't want us to tell you. But that doesn't seem fair to you.'

Cora could barely register the meaning of Ruby's words—all she could focus on was the fact that Rafael's arrival was imminent. The idea made her feel alive, filled her with excitement and fear and panic and joy.

The doorbell pealed and Ruby's sapphire gaze met hers. 'What do you want me to do? Do you want to see him?'

Indecisiveness added itself to the mix. Could she bear to see him? Could she bear not to?

'Yes… No…I don't know. I mean…did he say *why* he wants to see me?'

Ruby shook her head. 'He was very unforthcoming, despite my best efforts.'

'Then there's only one way to find out. I'll see him.'

Ruby nodded and then headed for the door. Cora rose to her feet and gripped the back of the chair for support, her fingers squishing into the soft material as she tried to calm the rocketing of her pulse.

The door opened and her heart stopped, started, skittered and eventually settled on a rhythm that threatened to rattle her ribcage.

'Rafael,' she said.

Rafael paused on the threshold, brought to a halt by the sheer impact of seeing Cora. He absorbed the beauty of her face, the glory of the red hair that cascaded to her shoulders, observed the smudges under her turquoise eyes, her extra slenderness accentuated by the simple dark green T-shirt and denim cut-offs she wore.

It took all his self-control not to stride forward and pull her into his arms. *Cool it, Martinez.* There was wariness in her expression, and the last thing he wanted was to spook her.

Then her gaze dropped from his as she spotted Dottie by his side. Her lips formed a circle of surprise before curving up into a smile as the large sandy-coloured dog trotted forward, sniffed Cora's out-turned hands, then sat in front of her and pawed her leg with a gentle stroke. Without reservation Cora sank to her haunches and the big dog rolled over for a tummy-rub, head lolling in sheer appreciation.

He stepped forward as Ruby and Ethan entered the room.

'Right,' Ruby said. 'We'll leave you two to it. If you

want lunch it's in the kitchen. Boeuf Bourgignon, wild rice and salad, and a bottle of Martinez plonk.'

Cora gave Dottie one last pat and rose to her feet. 'Thank you,' she said, with a touch of doubt in her voice—presumably as to what she was thanking them *for*.

As Ethan walked past he clapped Rafael on the shoulder. 'Good luck, mate—and don't blow it,' he murmured.

Easy for Ethan to say.

Once the Cavershams had departed silence descended. Rafael's thoughts were scrambled. His guts seethed with nerves and his legendary charm seemed to have legged it to faraway places.

'So...' Cora retreated back behind the dark red armchair. 'You took Dottie in?'

'Yes.' *Gold star for conversational ability, Martinez.*

'That's great. How's it working out?' She glanced down to where Dottie was crashed out at his feet. 'Not that I need to ask. It seems clear she has bonded.'

A sudden smile lit her face, then vanished, and he knew why—saw the concern in her eyes.

'I've bonded too. I would never have taken Dottie if it wasn't for ever.'

He could see the doubt etched in the crease of her forehead and he could hardly blame her. His remembered words on the subject of lifestyle and commitment swooped in to bite him royally on the behind.

'Cora. I promise. Dottie is a part of my life now.'

Until now he'd never understood how people could bond so completely with an animal. But from the moment he had picked Dottie up from Sally Anne he'd not once regretted it. This enormous soppy dog was full of a capacity to love, and Rafael had little doubt that she would guard him with her life if necessary. Full of character and independence, she had settled into his villa in La Rioja, loving the freedom of the local fields. Yet she also roamed the

vineyard at his heel. Equally, she seemed to have adapted
to his London home and in truth…

'I couldn't imagine life without her.'

For a long moment Cora studied his expression. Then,
as if satisfied by whatever she'd read, she gave a small nod.
'Good.' Her eyes narrowed and her knuckles whitened on
the back of the chair. 'So why are you here?'

'I needed to see you…to tell you…' *I love you.* 'I didn't
buy the Aiza vineyard.'

Jeez. What was the matter with him? *Fear.* He was ter-
rified to tell her how he felt in case she ran screaming from
the room—in case he lost her for ever.

Her forehead scrunched into that quintessentially Cora
frown and his fingers itched to smooth the creases.

'You didn't buy it? But you said… You… Why on earth
not?'

'I couldn't do it. I stood in Don Carlos's office and he
offered me his admiration for my marriage, for using you
to get a foothold into the higher echelons of society—using
you to gain his vineyard and future deals. And I couldn't
do it. I couldn't use you like that.'

Her turquoise eyes widened and she shook her head.
'Why not? I know how much that vineyard meant to you.'

'Not as much as you do.'

All the fear had gone now. Whatever the outcome for
himself, he wanted her to know he loved her.

'I love you, Cora. With all my heart and soul.'

Her face was illuminated—and then the frown returned.
'But…that doesn't make sense. I thought you didn't *do*
love. I thought you couldn't wait to be shot of me.'

'I definitely do love.'

He met her gaze full-on, hoped she could see the sincerity and love that blazed inside him.

'I think I've loved you since I took you to La Rioja and
saw through to the *real* Cora Derwent. The beautiful, pas-

sionate woman who sees good in people. The incredibly generous woman who cares and who has the most astounding capacity to love. I love you, Cora, and I don't want you to *ever* doubt that. Because I never will. You've changed me. I always swore I'd avoid love because I saw it as something that weakened you, gave someone else power over you, held you back from living life.'

'And now?'

'Now I know it doesn't have to be like that. I will still want to seize opportunities and live life to the full, but now I want to do that with you by my side. Now I see that love can make you a better person, give you strength and compassion, and that with love comes trust. Trust that you can work through the hard times, knowledge that being together is a million times better than being apart. You make me whole, Cora, and I love every hair on your head and every molecule of your being. I love your smile, and the way you scrunch your forehead up when you're thinking. I love being with you. And all I want is to wake up beside you every day for the rest of my life. I *love* you. You've made me see the world differently. Does that make sense?'

'Completely. Because I love you too. More than anything.'

Two strides brought him to the red armchair and she walked round it and straight into his arms. Elation and joy bubbled inside him—Cora loved him.

'Loving you has changed the way I see the world too. I believed you couldn't love a person like me—not when there are so many beautiful, talented women in the world. Because my parents made me believe that that's how love works. They loved Kaitlin and Gabe because of their looks and their talents—they couldn't love me because I wasn't beautiful or talented. But now I know love *doesn't* work like that. I love you because you're *you*, and these past two months I've missed you. I've missed your voice, our con-

versations, the way you make me feel alive, your touch…
I've missed *you. Everything* about you—your stubborn-
ness, your ability to seize the moment, the way you know
how to have fun but also care so deeply.'

Her beautiful smile curved her lips, lit her eyes with
joy.

'So I love you because you're you, and you love me because I'm me.'

'I couldn't have put it better myself. You've made me
a better person, Cora. Do you remember I told you about
my father?'

'Of course I remember.'

'What I didn't tell you was his identity. My father is
Ramon de Guzman, and my grandfather—the man who
terrorised my mother with his goons—is Don Carlos,
Duque de Aiza.'

Her lips parted in a small gasp. 'So *that's* why you
wanted the vineyard?'

'Yes. It felt fair on some level that some Aiza land
should come to *me*, and I knew that Don Carlos would
be horrified that his land had ended up in his illegitimate
grandson's hands. I dreamt of his face when I told him
who I was, showed him my success. Stood over him and
watched him realise that I held the power to plunge his
house into scandal. I savoured the idea of producing the
first batch of Martinez wine on his vineyard—I would
have named it "Lady Emma".'

Anger crossed Cora's beautiful features. 'He would have
deserved all that.'

'Yes, but in the past months I've come to realise I don't
want revenge any more. I don't want to torment my enemies. Because you were right to say that vengeance and
justice are two different things. If I avenged myself on Don
Carlos others would be affected. I would effectively block
Juanita and Alvaro from my life—and they are my half-

siblings. Then there's my father… My mother wanted me to forgive him so I decided to write to him.'

As he recounted the story to Cora he relived it himself. Ramon de Guzman had written back to request a meeting, and days later he had arrived at Rafael's Madrid apartment. He had entered his study and stood for a moment in the doorway. The sense of how surreal it had felt as they had faced each other was impossible to describe. Memories had flooded back and Rafael had been able to see a glimpse of the man his father had once been, to see bits of himself in the aquiline features and dark eyes, as his father spoke.

'Rafael. I have come to…to apologise. To you and to the memory of your mother. I did love her, with all my heart, and I have never loved another since. I loved you too. But I wasn't strong enough to stand up for that love and deny my duty.

'When my father told me he had arranged a marriage for me, to a woman of noble blood, I did try to refuse. In the end I told him about your mother and you. He explained to me the impossibility of marriage to your mother, convinced me that to marry her would be to wrong my family name, my heritage. He promised me that if I agreed never to see you both again he would sort everything out honourably. You would be provided for, given a house, an education, an allowance—you and your mother would want for nothing. And, God forgive me, I agreed.

'Until I got your letter I believed all had happened as he'd said. I should have known, I should have tried to find you, but I knew that if I saw your mother again I would be lost. How could I have that on my conscience? My poor wife…she has already endured a cold, loveless marriage. And my children, Alvaro and Juanita—I had to think of them too.'

Ramon Aiza had looked at him with a plea in his eyes.

'Now I know what really happened I am in your hands. I will acknowledge you to the world if that is what you wish.'

'*Is* that what you want?' Cora asked now.

'No. I can't see the point in wreaking that kind of pain on all and sundry. I told Ramon that I would like Alvaro and Juanita to know of my existence, and that if they wish to meet with me I would like that.'

Cora squeezed his hand. 'I think you did the right thing—what your mother would have wished. But I'm so sorry that you went through all that alone. I wish I could have been there for you.'

'It sounds mad, but in a way you were. I carried your image in my mind and in my heart.' He reached into his pocket. 'But now I want more than that. I want to spend the rest of my life with the real flesh and blood you.' As he pulled the jeweller's box from his pocket he sank to one knee and looked up at her. 'Will you marry me for real, Cora Derwent?'

'Yes, Rafael Martinez, I will. Yes, with all my heart.'

He slipped the ring onto her finger and saw her face light up as she gazed down at the blue turquoise set in gold. Not a diamond in sight. Because now he understood their connotations for her, so he had chosen a rare form of turquoise to match her eyes—a ring designed and chosen with love, not for show.

'It's beautiful,' she breathed as he rose to his feet. 'I am honoured to wear it.'

One final qualm assailed him. 'But your parents…they won't be happy about this.'

'That's up to them. You told me that I changed you for the better—well, you have done the same for me. Loving you gave me the strength to stand up to my parents, because I realised I didn't want to win their approval at the cost of losing my self-respect. I can't sacrifice my life or my principles to gain their love. If they love me they have to love the real Cora. And if they decide to disown me because I marry you then so be it. It's their loss. I love you and you love me.'

And now the joy remained on her face, illuminating it with a glow of such happiness that it was impossible to doubt her sincerity.

'And I want us to feel good about that love and proclaim it to the world. I won't do what Ramon did and let my family's misguided notions dictate my happiness. Or yours.' Stepping into the warm circle of his arms, she smiled up at him. 'I want to live my life to the very fullest, with you by my side.'

Happiness banded his chest, and as he kissed her Rafael Martinez took the greatest opportunity of all—to love and be loved in return.

EPILOGUE

CORA WATCHED THE shadow and light from the September sun dapple the villa floor, inhaled the heavy harvest scent as it wafted through the open windows from the nearby vineyard.

'How do I look this time?' she asked Kaitlin.

'Stunning. This dress is perfect.'

Cora had to agree—she adored the dress she had chosen for the renewal of their wedding vows. Long and flowing, it fell in pools of white round her feet, whilst the transparent neckline with its pretty floral pattern round her shoulders gave it a fairytale touch.

'But it's not only the dress, Sis. It's you. You glow with happiness.'

'That's what love does,' Cora said. 'I seem to radiate joy.'

Every morning she woke up with her heart full of wonder and thanks as she reached out to feel the solid strength of her husband next to her.

Then she saw her sister's expression, heavy with despair. 'Kait, what's wrong?'

'Nothing. I'm fine.'

'No, you're not.'

Cora had seen more of her sister in the past months than she had since their childhood. Kaitlin had given both public and private support to her decision to remain married to Rafael, and had helped win her parents' grudging acceptance of the union—though they had declined to attend this simple renewal ceremony.

'Tell me what's wrong, Kait. Maybe I can help. Is it Prince Frederick?'

Kaitlin pressed her lips together. 'Please don't worry—I will sort it out. Really, I will. And if I need help I'll come to you. I promise.'

'I'll hold you to that. But, Kait, don't marry Frederick unless you love him.'

Her sister shook her head. 'Come on. Now isn't the time.'

Cora nodded and led the way out to the vineyard. She beamed at the scattering of guests. There was Juanita, who had welcomed the advent of Rafael into her life, and Ethan and Ruby, on the cusp of parenthood—they had been approved as adopters just the previous week. And there stood Gabe, whom Kaitlin had managed to track down—though he refused to discuss where he'd been or why, or what he'd been doing—arms folded, his hazel eyes watchful. María and Tomás stood arm in arm and the three dogs—Dottie, Prue and Poppy—lay at their feet, their coats gleaming in the Spanish sunshine.

And most important of all there was Rafael—her rock, her partner and her soulmate.

Her heart skipped as she walked towards him without hesitation, saw his smile light his face with happiness. As she reached him and he took her hands in his she knew that their love would endure the test of time, and she looked forward with all her heart and soul to spending the rest of her life with this wonderful man—this time each word of their vows would resonate with truth and love.

* * * * *

MILLS & BOON®
Hardback – May 2016

ROMANCE

Morelli's Mistress	Anne Mather
A Tycoon to Be Reckoned With	Julia James
Billionaire Without a Past	Carol Marinelli
The Shock Cassano Baby	Andie Brock
The Most Scandalous Ravensdale	Melanie Milburne
The Sheikh's Last Mistress	Rachael Thomas
Claiming the Royal Innocent	Jennifer Hayward
Kept at the Argentine's Command	Lucy Ellis
The Billionaire Who Saw Her Beauty	Rebecca Winters
In the Boss's Castle	Jessica Gilmore
One Week with the French Tycoon	Christy McKellen
Rafael's Contract Bride	Nina Milne
Tempted by Hollywood's Top Doc	Louisa George
Perfect Rivals...	Amy Ruttan
English Rose in the Outback	Lucy Clark
A Family for Chloe	Lucy Clark
The Doctor's Baby Secret	Scarlet Wilson
Married for the Boss's Baby	Susan Carlisle
Twins for the Texan	Charlene Sands
Secret Baby Scandal	Joanne Rock

MILLS & BOON®
Large Print – May 2016

ROMANCE

The Queen's New Year Secret	Maisey Yates
Wearing the De Angelis Ring	Cathy Williams
The Cost of the Forbidden	Carol Marinelli
Mistress of His Revenge	Chantelle Shaw
Theseus Discovers His Heir	Michelle Smart
The Marriage He Must Keep	Dani Collins
Awakening the Ravensdale Heiress	Melanie Milburne
His Princess of Convenience	Rebecca Winters
Holiday with the Millionaire	Scarlet Wilson
The Husband She'd Never Met	Barbara Hannay
Unlocking Her Boss's Heart	Christy McKellen

HISTORICAL

In Debt to the Earl	Elizabeth Rolls
Rake Most Likely to Seduce	Bronwyn Scott
The Captain and His Innocent	Lucy Ashford
Scoundrel of Dunborough	Margaret Moore
One Night with the Viking	Harper St. George

MEDICAL

A Touch of Christmas Magic	Scarlet Wilson
Her Christmas Baby Bump	Robin Gianna
Winter Wedding in Vegas	Janice Lynn
One Night Before Christmas	Susan Carlisle
A December to Remember	Sue MacKay
A Father This Christmas?	Louisa Heaton

MILLS & BOON®
Hardback – June 2016

ROMANCE

Bought for the Greek's Revenge	Lynne Graham
An Heir to Make a Marriage	Abby Green
The Greek's Nine-Month Redemption	Maisey Yates
Expecting a Royal Scandal	Caitlin Crews
Return of the Untamed Billionaire	Carol Marinelli
Signed Over to Santino	Maya Blake
Wedded, Bedded, Betrayed	Michelle Smart
The Surprise Conti Child	Tara Pammi
The Greek's Nine-Month Surprise	Jennifer Faye
A Baby to Save Their Marriage	Scarlet Wilson
Stranded with Her Rescuer	Nikki Logan
Expecting the Fellani Heir	Lucy Gordon
The Prince and the Midwife	Robin Gianna
His Pregnant Sleeping Beauty	Lynne Marshall
One Night, Twin Consequences	Annie O'Neil
Twin Surprise for the Single Doc	Susanne Hampton
The Doctor's Forbidden Fling	Karin Baine
The Army Doc's Secret Wife	Charlotte Hawkes
A Pregnancy Scandal	Kat Cantrell
A Bride for the Boss	Maureen Child

MILLS & BOON®
Large Print – June 2016

ROMANCE

Leonetti's Housekeeper Bride	Lynne Graham
The Surprise De Angelis Baby	Cathy Williams
Castelli's Virgin Widow	Caitlin Crews
The Consequence He Must Claim	Dani Collins
Helios Crowns His Mistress	Michelle Smart
Illicit Night with the Greek	Susanna Carr
The Sheikh's Pregnant Prisoner	Tara Pammi
Saved by the CEO	Barbara Wallace
Pregnant with a Royal Baby!	Susan Meier
A Deal to Mend Their Marriage	Michelle Douglas
Swept into the Rich Man's World	Katrina Cudmore

HISTORICAL

Marriage Made in Rebellion	Sophia James
A Too Convenient Marriage	Georgie Lee
Redemption of the Rake	Elizabeth Beacon
Saving Marina	Lauri Robinson
The Notorious Countess	Liz Tyner

MEDICAL

Playboy Doc's Mistletoe Kiss	Tina Beckett
Her Doctor's Christmas Proposal	Louisa George
From Christmas to Forever?	Marion Lennox
A Mummy to Make Christmas	Susanne Hampton
Miracle Under the Mistletoe	Jennifer Taylor
His Christmas Bride-to-Be	Abigail Gordon

0516 GEN STD LP